MY
REFORMED
ROGUE

COPYRIGHT

CHAPTER
ONE

"Yah!" Lady Anwen Astoridge drove her robust sixteen-hand mare into a canter, leaning forward in the saddle and urging her over a high hedge grove.

The wind whipped at her hair, the last of the pins her maid had strategically and carefully placed only hours before fell to the ground, lost forever in the muddy field. Her bottle-green riding suit, splattered with leaves and mud, modeled perfectly against her figure, even if she was no longer fit to be seen.

Should her mama see her, she would have apoplexy and scream down the house, demanding her brother keep a better handle on his wayward sister's soul. But Dominic would not. He loved her and allowed her to enjoy what life had to offer.

And right at this moment, it offered a day away from home, riding the hundreds of acres they owned and enjoying a picnic in solitude, if the weather held clear and warm.

Anwen pulled Luna into a slow trot before walking the remainder quarter mile to the fast-flowing river on their land's outskirts. A place she had found and called her own for many years now. A place she had not even shown her twin sister, so much she wished it to remain the one place on earth she could sit and ponder, think, and plan.

How to get out of the London Season in particular.

She frowned, knowing that her latest ruse would only last so long. As far as her family understood, she was still abed, resting after an atrocious summer cold.

And while all of that was true, she may have prolonged her cough and symptoms far longer than they deserved. But what joy consumed her the day she watched her sister ride off toward London with her mama, brother, and new sister-in-law in tow while she remained at Nettingvale.

A ruse she knew would not last forever.

The sound of water rushing over rocks drifted through the copse of trees, and she dismounted, loosened the reins for Luna, allowing her to graze, and strode with her satchel bag toward the river.

The sight of her little oasis brought a smile to her lips, and she settled on her flat rock, rummaging through the satchel in search of what Mrs. Florence had packed for lunch.

The poor servants were not as pleased with Anwen prolonging her illness. She was under no illusion they all knew she was now playing her family for fools, but they would also not dare tell a viscount's sister that she was placing her pretty slippered feet on the wrong side of the boards and being devilish.

She unwrapped the slice of pie and took a bite, closing her eyes as the taste of raspberries, and Mrs. Florence's sweet pastry, burst into her mouth. The lady was a true master of delicious food. She really ought to be more than a viscount's cook.

Of course, her ruse would not last forever. There was little doubt her brother, maybe even tomorrow, would send a letter demanding answers regarding her health, and the housekeeper would apprise him, and she too would be soon shipped off to town.

How she hoped the letter was delayed as much as possible or, better yet, would never arrive. Maybe if she could intercept it...

"Good afternoon," a male voice said from across the river.

Anwen jumped at the intrusion, almost choking on her pie, before she swallowed and skimmed the trees on the opposite bank, looking for the elusive voice.

Typically Anwen was not one to succumb to a pretty face, but even she felt her eyebrows rise and her eyes widen at the sight of the man before her.

A very tall, rugged, broad-shouldered man with a head full of curls that cascaded over his ears and nape as if they could never be tamed.

She shut her mouth with a snap and schooled her features to one of lofty disdain. If one needed to remove a person one did not know or seek the company off, the cut direct was what she ought to do.

However, that would have been far easier had he not had the most infectious grin on his lips.

He indeed appeared harmless enough.

"Perhaps you did not hear me, miss, but I wished to say hello. I'm—"

"I know who you are," she blurted, taking in his ragged attire, possibly more mud splattered than hers. Indeed, he appeared to be of the working class. She cast her eyes past him and saw his horse, a beautiful creature much like hers, and his identity became clear. "You must be the new Lord

Orford's groom. I heard he was traveling to Surrey soon, and much of his staff as well, now that he's finally bothered to move into the estate he inherited." She bit into the last of her pie, watching him as she savored the final morsel.

"Well, I suppose his living in London did delay him..." the servant hedged.

"What's the new marquess like?" she cut in, not caring about his life in London. Nothing of interest ever happened in that city. "Can you tell me? I heard he's young and did not expect to inherit." She chuckled at her musings. "Is he literate, do you know? Some say he came from such a distant line of the family that he had no learning."

The groom's face blanched before he cleared his throat, thinking about her question. Anwen had to credit him for keeping his cool after her prodding and teasing, but that was all it was. How much easier it was to find out information about a person when making assumptions that were incorrect in the first place.

People always were more than willing to correct inaccurate assumptions.

"He is literate. I can assure you, miss."

"Lady Anwen Astoridge, mister..." she asked.

"Mr. Clarence at your service and Lord Orford's too, I suppose," he said, bowing. "But you already guessed that."

She reached into her satchel for the bottle of lemonade Cook had sent with her.

"I suppose this is where you tell me we should not speak to each other since I'm a lowly groom and you're a lady." He glanced about before walking to a rock, much situated like her own, and sat.

She shrugged, having never been high in the instep, even if her teasing said otherwise. In fact, she knew all her brother's servants by their first names and many of their family members and ensured that whenever a problem arose, they must come to her and the family as soon as they were comfortable so they could help.

"I can sit and speak to you. There is no harm in that." She poured herself a drink. "You do not look like the type of man who would do me harm, and my horse is quick, and I'm a good rider. You would need to be swift to catch me should you attempt a foray."

Mr. Clarence burst into laughter, wiping his eyes before he could form a response. "For a lady, you speak very frankly, I must say."

"And for a groom, you speak very formally. Are you sure you're a servant?" she asked, unsure if that were the case. Maybe the new Marquess of Orford educated his staff. It would certainly make him a much more favorable neighbor than the late marquess, who was a cranky, old recluse.

"I have not lied about my name, I assure you, but I am new to this area, as is the Marquess of Orford. I have not seen you before this day, so I can safely assume you have not met your new neighbor?" he asked.

Anwen shook her head, wishing she had, if only to have something to write to her twin sister Kate about. "No, I have not met him ever. All we know is that the late Lord Orford passed in his sleep over a year ago and had no heir except for a distant relative. With you sitting before me, I suppose we can now assume the new Lord Orford is in residence. What is he like, truly?" she asked, curious if the rumors regarding the marquess were true.

But if there was one fault Anwen had, it was that of being nosy and asking far too many questions when they were not necessarily polite or the time to do so.

"He is a good man, honest, although prone to pranks that not everyone thinks are amusing."

"How sad for people not to laugh when one is funny or says something amusing. A droll life, would you not agree?"

"I would indeed agree." He smiled, and something in the pit of Anwen's stomach fluttered. How handsome and polite this groom was. What a shame he was not of her ranking, where she would be allowed to get to know him better.

"You speak very well. The marquess has invested in your education, I assume. Another admirable quality that the ladies in London will most certainly appreciate. Charity and looking after one's servants is honorable."

A look of disdain crossed his features before he met her eyes. "I was well educated, but due to my father's tireless devotion to making me the best man I could be. Lord Orford will merely benefit from my father's tutelage."

"I'm happy for you, but may I be so bold as to ask why you're working as his lordship's groom if you're so well educated? Maybe you should have been a steward, furthered your education, and became a lawyer or doctor."

"I love horses and cannot think of anything more I wish to tend to in my life." He gestured to her mount grazing not far from where she sat. "Your horse, Lady Anwen, is a beauty. Do you ride her often?"

"Most days and here always," she said, dismissing the thought as to why she needed to tell him that tidbit of information. "I, too, enjoy the pastime."

"So we have something in common, no matter our difference in social spheres," he said, his infectious grin making her smile.

She supposed they did.

CHAPTER
TWO

L ord Daniel Clarence, Marquess of Orford ought to do the right thing and explain how Lady Anwen Astoridge had leaped to the wrong conclusions and had his identity incorrect.

A groom indeed...not that he hadn't wished at times that he could live such a carefree, easy life as the one she believed him to be living. Inheriting the Orford title was by no means a little occasion, and many were expecting him to fail, him most of all.

He was not known to be the most honorable or fair man on English soil or the easiest to get along with, but he hoped he did not ruin the estate and the living that had landed in his fortunate lap.

That his neighbor was Lady Anwen was a promising turn of events, especially since he knew the young woman's brother. Or at least, there had been a time when their paths crossed at Eton when his parents thought to try to educate him for a month or two.

He moved closer to the water and sat, kicking off his boots and stockings and slipping his feet into the chilled stream. A refreshing moment and a pleasant one, considering the vision that was before him.

Lady Anwen was one of the most handsome women he had ever seen. Her riding habit hinted at a woman's developed body, ample bosom, and an ideal shape to her ass.

He licked his lips and cautioned himself against acting the rogue. He was a groom, after all, not a man on equal footing as her ladyship before him, or so she thought. He could not toy with the chit.

As much as he wished he could.

"What else do you have in your satchel, Lady Anwen? Care to share?" he boldly asked, noting her eyes widened at his request, but instead of criticizing him, she merely rummaged in her bag and pulled out a small, wrapped piece of food.

Without warning, she threw it across the stream, and he caught it, the scent of cooked chicken permeating the air. "Oh, thank you very much. Whatever this is smells divine."

She busied herself with her wrapped food, not bothering to look his way. "It's just bread with chicken. Our cook prepared it for me and other tasty things, although why she prepared two, I do not know."

"Maybe she had an inkling that your fate would change today, and you would meet a dark, handsome stranger."

"You're neither dark nor handsome, sir." She narrowed her eyes on him. "In any case, you should probably eat with haste. I would not think grooms would have an overly long lunch break."

He chuckled. He could have as long as he wished, not that he would tell her such a truth, not when she was being so honest and open. "I shall return soon to the estate. Now that I've met you, I do not wish to lose my employment. However, I may if we meet here again and I am caught."

"And what a shame that would be." The indifference in her words was not lost on him. How delightful this day had turned since he had fled his house only an hour before, needing the air and space away from the mess his distant relative had left the estate. A man he had never met. Something he was glad of once he knew how and what he had been doing to the estate all these years.

"Admit it, Lady Anwen, your day is far brighter after meeting me. You can return to your home and have more of an understanding of how us lowly workers labor on your grand estates."

She raised one criticizing eyebrow. "Are you calling me an elitist, Mr. Clarence?"

"Do you feel like a snobbish prig? I suppose I ought to give you credit since you have given me part of your lunch." He bit back a laugh when she stared at him as if he had lost his mind.

"If I were so high in the instep, I would neither speak to you nor share my food with you. An oddity, since this is your lunch break, one would think you would have your own fare. But in any case, should I be like so many of my sex, I would not even be here in Surrey. I'd be in London with my sister and family enjoying the height of the Season. But I am not."

"Curious. You have me intrigued. Do explain why it is that you're here and not in London." He bit into the bread with chicken that Lady Anwen had thrown to him and groaned. The Astoridge cook was a marvel and put his elderly male chef to shame. Maybe he ought to call on the Astoridge estate and offer the servant a wage she could not refuse.

"I should not say," she hedged, taking a healthy bite of her food herself and halting the ability to form a reply.

He waited for her to swallow, taking the opportunity to watch her mouth, and full lips, as she chewed. What a pretty little chit she was. No, that wasn't correct. She was far from a chit; she was a young woman, bursting free of her youthful follies and stepping forth into her future. She would marry, of course, some highly placed lord who would breed babies off her body, ignoring her during the day and using her at night. The thought left a sour taste in his mouth, and he glanced out into the wooded lands, not wanting to imagine such a benign future that held no fire and fun that she so obviously enjoyed.

A woman who picnicked alone beside a river with a magnificent horse like the one she was riding was not afraid of life or excitement for what was next.

They could have a lot of fun together if she allowed it.

Not that he should allow it. He was not the marrying type.

"Come now, are we not friends? And who better to tell your secrets than a lowly groom who has no one to tell anything to in the first place?"

For several minutes she did not speak, and he was about to give up on knowing why she was still in Surrey and not London when she finally hedged to talk.

"I suppose it would not signify to tell you. It is not as if you'll write a letter to my brother and out my secret."

"Of course not," he said, laying his hand across his chest for good measure.

She pursed her lips, and again, he was reminded how kissable they were. Not that she seemed at all aware of how striking she was...

"I will say in my defense that I did not plan what eventually transpired at first, but I was ill of late. I caught a cold that settled on my chest and would not relent. The date for us all to leave for London grew ever closer, and yet I was not well enough to leave with my family. Or so my brother thought. I was well enough, but pretended not to be to remain at home. I have no interest in London or finding a husband. Not right now, in any case."

He frowned, having not expected her to be such an actress. Nor could he understand how she did not enjoy London. He loved the city, the bustling, the whores... "And your brother bought your ruse regarding your prolonged illness. I'm surprised they left you behind."

"Well, at first, they were not going to, but I convinced them that within a week or two, I would return to my healthy self once more and join them. That time is almost up, but I'm loath to leave. So I've had to send letters explaining that I'm still too unwell for the hours-long carriage ride. I hope to remain here at Nettingvale for several more weeks at least. Maybe I'll even be able to avoid the Season altogether."

"Unlikely," he scoffed. "From what I know of brothers and their sisters who are debuting in London, they want them married and settled as soon as may be." He paused, not wanting to give himself away. "Your brother recently married, did he not?" At her nod, he continued. "Well, all the more reason to have his sisters married."

"I did not tell you I had a sister, Mr. Clarence," she said, her eyes narrowing on him.

"I'm the groom of your neighbor, the marquess. I know the family dynamics, Lady Anwen. I assure you there is no mystery in my words," he said, hoping his explanation settled her fears and cursing himself a liar at the same time. Another trait he was far from proud of.

Her bored sigh seemed to state that it did. "I know I must travel to London soon, but maybe not for some weeks. I want to stay here in Surrey. I'm far too young to marry."

"I could not agree more." He took the last bite of his food and placed the rubbish in his pocket.

"How old is the new marquess? Very little is known of him," she asked, surprising him that she would care to learn. But he supposed he was new to the area and an unknown. People were bound to be curious.

"He's a young lord, Lady Anwen, but a dreadful bore, not refined as much as the ladies would like, and a little bit of a scoundrel, or so I've heard." He let that last tidbit of information hover between them; waiting for her to ask more if she wished.

She bit her lip, and a warm knot churned in his stomach for the first time in eons. "Now I'm curious, Mr. Clarence. Mayhap, you should explain what you mean by that."

Now he'd done it.

THREE

"Alas, Lady Anwen, I cannot say more than I have already. It would be unkind to an excellent master if I were to elaborate." Mr. Clarence slapped his knees with his hands and stood.

Anwen watched him. His leaving before he told her a little of their new neighbor seemed ungentlemanly of him. But then, he did have a point. As the new marquess's groom, his loyalty should be with Lord Orford and not herself and her growing need for succulent gossip.

"I suppose I can assume you're leaving, Mr. Clarence," she said, standing also. The afternoon was waning, and the sun had disappeared several times behind gray clouds, cooling the air significantly. No matter how much she pretended to be ill to avoid London, she did not actually wish to grow sick with the ague again.

"I must," he said, bending into a gallant bow. "But something tells me that we shall meet again. At least I hope to," he teased, a wicked light in his eyes that ought not to be there. He was a groom, for heaven's sake. She should not be employing or encouraging such wayward speech. But then, he was so very handsome. There was a ruggedness about Mr. Clarence that was often lost on the lords and gentlemen in her society. They preened a lot, glanced far too often in mirrors for her liking, and she did not want a husband who needed to appear more fashionable or striking than his wife.

Not to mention gentlemen were untrustworthy, as she, unfortunately, found out after her first Season in town.

Not that she could think such things concerning the man before her, no matter how much he appealed. He was a groom, and she was a viscount's sister. The difference in their social spheres was too great ever to meld.

"Well, should I see you on my daily rides, I'll be sure to say hello. And do pass on our regards to Lord Orford and welcome him to the county. When my brother returns from town, we'll invite his lordship for dinner."

"I should imagine he would welcome such an invitation, Lady Anwen." Mr. Clarence set his foot in the stirrup and pulled himself up on his horse, turning it toward the Orford Estate. "Good day to you, Lady Anwen. It has been a pleasure."

She smiled, liking the thought that her company had brought him delight. "Likewise," she boldly said. "Good afternoon."

With one last glance, he kicked his mount and cantered away. Anwen watched him go, enjoying the sight of Mr. Clarence's backside in the saddle. Maybe she should have gone to London if the view of the groom's backside made her think things no lady of her position should.

Her mama would have apoplexy should she learn she had spent the afternoon with a groom, and unchaperoned.

She frowned at the thought. Possibly, not her finest or wisest choice of company, but no one would ever know or find out. She doubted Mr. Clarence would exclaim his afternoon to fellow servants. To do so seemed an odd thing to do.

Anwen turned on her heel and packed her picnic in her travel bag before walking her horse to a large boulder and climbing up into the saddle.

Tomorrow she would ride again, possibly even farther afield. A pretty view from one of her brother's hills enabled one to see the Orford estate. Maybe she would come across Mr. Clarence again? Perhaps she would see the new marquess.

All coincidence should they cross paths again. A lady such as she would never seek the company of a servant. That was not how she was brought up, even if the thought sent butterflies in her stomach to flutter.

The following morning Anwen woke late, bathed, and sent a message to the stables to have her horse saddled at once. She would not picnic today, but check on several boundary hedge groves of her brother's estate to ensure everything was as it should be.

She would hate for any of their livestock to get out and cause strife for their neighbors...

After breaking her fast, it wasn't long before she was again attired in her bottle-green riding habit, cantering out of the horse yard and heading into the fields surrounding the home.

The day was as perfect as yesterday, apart from a few clouds that could prove troublesome later in the afternoon. The crisp morning air revitalized her and beckoned the adventure she longed for.

Anwen marveled at how fortunate she was. Not

everyone had a charmed life like the one she led, and she was more than aware of how blessed they all were, especially after her brother's marriage to Paris, who saved them all from financial ruin.

Not that she never wished to marry, but after her disappointing last Season, she didn't want to rush into such an important decision. Her poor brother would soon learn that she would not be so easy to walk down the aisle as her sister would be.

Not that she did not like gentlemen; that was far from the truth. The vision of Mr. Clarence came to mind, and he was undoubtedly a man she found attractive and one she wished to know more about. Even if he were not the marrying type, not for her, at least.

But one day, some lady in his social sphere would be fortunate to have him as a husband.

She pushed her horse to quicken her pace up a lane, and she was soon cantering toward the hill that gave a good view of the Orford estate. Was Mr. Clarence up already, working horses in the stable yards, or maybe he was mucking out their stalls, refilling water, brushing the marquess's horses?

The new marquess had undoubtedly brought all his horses with him to Orford House. His stablehands would be busy indeed settling in the new stock.

She pulled her horse to a stop at the top of the hill and, reaching into her saddlebag, took out a pair of binoculars. Raising them, she focused on the Orford House, moving from the house to where she believed the stable block was located.

A gardener walked a cart onto the lawn, several tools lying within it. A maid leaned out a second-floor window, brushing down and freeing the stonework of cobwebs and leaves.

There was, she supposed, quite a lot of activity on the estate. The now-deceased marquess was not known for being houseproud, nor had she ever heard of his lordship holding a ball or dinner in all her years.

A recluse from all accounts, and having not seen hide nor hair of the new marquess, she couldn't help but wonder if he wasn't the same.

"What are we looking at today? Anything happening of interest?"

Anwen squealed, and her horse took several steps back at her exclamation.

Heat prickled over her body, crawling up her neck to settle on her cheeks. Mortified, she met the laughing gaze of Mr. Clarence. Oh dear Lord, he had seen her ogling the estate like some crazed zealot. What would he think of her?

"Mr. Clarence. I did not hear you approach." A weak excuse for being caught watching his employer's estate, but the only one she could come up with at that moment.

He chuckled and stole the binoculars from her fingers, raising them to his eyes and turning them on the estate she was ogling.

"Hmm, yes, not much transpiring, I see. However, some staff are working hard to clean up the estate. The stables are in a terrible state. I really ought to be down there mucking them out with everyone else."

Anwen had to agree. Anywhere but here, watching her blush at being caught red-handed being nosy.

"I'm sorry for spying. I'm merely curious about the new marquess," she lied, knowing she was not, in truth, watching the house to find the marquess. She would have enjoyed catching a glimpse of the man next to her.

Just not next *to* her.

"I'm sure his lordship is still abed," he quipped, handing back her binoculars, which she promptly threw into her saddle bag. Dear Lord, whatever would he think of her?

"But I see you're up and riding on my brother's land." She raised her brow, needing to feel superior after feeling nothing but a fool.

He grinned and nodded in agreement. "I saw you from Lord Orford's land and thought to come to see you. We are friends, are we not, or was I wrong in thinking so? Perhaps you think me too lowly to be your friend, Lady Anwen."

Something about his question told Anwen not to lie or joke about why they ought not to be friends or why she could not be his friend.

She wanted to be his friend no matter his station or hers.

"I do not think that, Mr. Clarence. Far from it, in fact."

CHAPTER
FOUR

There was something different about Lady Anwen that Daniel could not grasp, but he would enjoy spending time with the young woman to find out.

He ought not to smile at the unfortunate event of being caught spying on his estate, but he could not help it. Never had a woman, of rank or otherwise, been seen doing such antics, and it tickled a part of him that had long forgotten how to laugh.

He was not a man who played the doting rogue. Far easier to have a mistress, have her at his beck and call, and forgo all the niceties that ladies of rank thought they wanted during courtship.

Even if he did have a talent for flattery, he rarely needed to use such words. Money spoke far louder with the women who kept him company; they did not care for compliments so long as a gold coin was in his hand at the end of the evening.

But Lady Anwen would be different. The decision was whether he would wish to be different with her too and play this little game.

He took in her form as she steadfastly looked over her horse's ears, anywhere but at him after being caught so shamefully watching his estate.

He should tell her the truth about who he was and apologize for misleading her, but he did not want their casual, carefree interludes to end. Would she be so informal with him if she knew he was Lord Orford? He did not think that would be the case, and what a shame that would be.

Her bosom rose and fell with each breath, and a sweet rosy hue kissed her skin above her fichu. He would love to pluck that small piece of lace from her gown and throw it aside to see her better.

The rogue within him growled, and he pushed aside the need that grew from her beauty.

He could not let the vices that so long ruled his life before becoming a lord raise their seedy heads now.

"Do not worry, Lady Anwen. I shall not tell the marquess of what I came across this morning. Your secret is safe with me, so long as you do something for me in return."

She glanced at him, a curious light in her blue eyes, and for a moment, he lost himself in her striking gaze. Before he became a marquess, not many people were interested in his well-being or his words, so for a woman he hardly knew to seem genuinely interested in what he said next was heady indeed.

"And what is that, Mr. Clarence?" she asked.

He adjusted his seat, unsure why his heart beat fast. "Ride with me. There are some wonderful fields and hedge groves to jump, and I have not had a good run for some time. Not on this new estate. You could show me around your brother's home. I'm most curious."

Which was not entirely untrue. He was inquisitive to see how Lord Astoridge lived these days. His memory of him from Eton was hazy at best, but many years had passed since then. It was utterly coincidental that he had inherited a property that abuts the viscount's own.

"Of course, it would be a pleasure. Come," she said, not waiting a moment longer before she kicked her mount and was trotting down the hill before him.

Rogue that he was, Daniel watched her bottom bounce up and down several times on the saddle before following.

They rode for some time through fields, stopping to meet several of her brother's tenant farmers. Lady Anwen seemed comfortable with people, regardless of their status or wealth, and knew the children's names and what ailments had bothered them this past winter.

You should not play with her, Daniel, she's a kind soul...

They returned to the stream where they had first met, and she pulled to a stop before a long flat field, hedge groves in the far distance.

"Would you like to race, Mr. Clarence? This field leads back to Lord Orford's estate, and I shall soon have you home, but a good fast sprint, I always find, ends an afternoon of riding most pleasantly."

"Are you allowed to race, Lady Anwen?" He did not want her injuring herself or her horse, and she was, for all her love of the outdoors, a noblewoman.

She raised a haughty brow, reminding him of the ladies of the *ton*, too high in the instep and judging people on their wealth and titles instead of personal merit. How he hated that life and the fickleness, fakeness of it all. That he was now part of that world, no longer able to live adjacent to it... His former situation would be a lifestyle he would mourn. Now he was a man destined to marry a lady just like Anwen. A future he'd never thought would come to fruition.

"I'll have you know that I'm the most accomplished rider in my family. Few can best me, not even a marquess's groom."

He whistled, laughing at her challenge. "Oh, you are advocating for yourself most confidently. Maybe we should up the wager since you are certain you will win."

The smile whispering on her lips sent heat to his groin. God damn it, she was utterly charming and so damn pretty that he ached where he ought not. Even when she had moments of judging him, she made his blood simmer.

"A wager? What kind are you thinking, Mr. Clarence?"

The kind that she would not allow. The kind that would mean taking her sweet face in hand and kissing those delectable lips. To hear her sighs of delight, taste and savor her in ways no man ought unless she was his wife.

"You may choose the wager," he stated, deciding to act the gentleman. Perhaps for the first time in his life.

A *sk for your first kiss, Anwen!*
The thought battered against her skull, and she fought not to spew the words out into the open where she could never rip them back.

But she would not. She was a viscount's sister. She was a woman of nobility and could not ask a neighbor's groom to kiss her. No matter how much she may wish to.

But oh, how she wished to.

How utterly delightful Mr. Clarence was. Charming and amusing, with a wicked little temperament about his character that meant he would never be a bore.

But his mouth had occupied her thoughts most of this day. How it would be to forget all about who she was and how she had been brought up. All the rules and etiquette lessons that had been drilled into her from the moment she stopped dribbling as a babe.

How freeing would it be to give over to emotion, to need for the first time in her life? Not that she did not often have freedom, she tasted such a life whenever she was out riding on the lands with no one to criticize her, correct her posture, or ensure she spoke to those she must due to her station.

"I shall have to think upon it, Mr. Clarence, and I will tell you what I desire at the end of our race." At the groom's raised brow, she adjusted her seat and shortened the reins in her hands. "Are you ready? The first one over the hedge grove wins," she said.

"Very good, Lady Anwen. On your mark."

"Go!" she shouted.

And they were off.

Sensing a race, her horse did not dally but jumped forward, eating up the ground with toe-curling speed. Anwen sat low and forward in her saddle, the sight of Mr. Clarence out of her peripheral view telling her he was a stride behind.

The wind whipped at her hair, her long curls falling from their pins and spilling down her back. Her eyes watered at the speed with which they rode, and she laughed, unable to hold back the glee at their impromptu race.

She heard Mr. Clarence urge his horse faster, but her mare had something Mr. Clarence did not. A racing background and a win at Newmarket before retirement. She doubted the new marquess would have such fine horse stock.

The hedge grove grew bigger before them, and she adjusted her seat, readying herself to jump the short hedge. Her horse cleared the fence with little effort, but a harrowing curse that shouted from behind her told her Mr. Clarence did not have the same success.

She pulled her horse to a stop and turned about, trotting back to where her Mr. Clarence was sprawled in the muddy field, his horse on the other side of the hedge grove watching them as if questioning their senses of trying to make the horse jump such a hurdle.

Fear curdled in her stomach, and she jumped from her mount, kneeling in the mud, heedless of the mess of her riding habit and what a horrible time her maid would have getting the muck out of her gown.

"Mr. Clarence, can you speak? Are you well? Are you hurt?" She cradled his face, careful not to move his head, and leaned over him. "Speak to me. Tell me if I should fetch help," she asked.

He sighed and opened his eyes, and that wicked, playful grin lifted his kissable lips. "Only my pride and my arse is injured, Lady Anwen. But I think I should lay here for a little longer until the embarrassment of being beaten by a woman and thrown from my horse wears off."

She chuckled, leaning back on her heels. "You still owe me my prize. I did win, after all."

"What do you want?" he asked, his voice dipping to a seductive fashion she'd never heard him speak. The depth of his tone sent a ball of heat low in her belly. He held her gaze, making her more flummoxed than she'd ever been.

"I think I wish for a kiss," she said.

He sat up, startling her with his speed. "A kiss? Well, I can undoubtedly do that."

"I knew you could," she said, giving him her hand. "On the back of my glove, will do just fine."

CHAPTER FIVE

T he look on Mr. Clarence's face was a mixture of shock and awe, and Anwen laughed, wiggling her fingers before his face until he took her hand and kissed her as she asked.

That was where the amusement of the situation fled.

The feel of his warm, gloveless hands touching hers, even though she *was* wearing gloves, was not what she expected. A bolt of energy shot through her fingers and up her arm, settling in her belly. Her eyes met his as his lips lingered scandalously on the top of her hand. Anwen drew a startled breath. Dear Lord in Heaven, he was unlike any man she had ever met.

The determination in his eyes made her regret asking for a kiss in such a benign place. When a man looked at a woman like Mr. Clarence was, as if he wanted to do more than kiss her glove, as if he wanted to drag her into his arms and kiss her soundly, denying such a need was difficult.

He's a groom, Anwen. Do not be absurd.

She pulled away and schooled her features. She would not be a silly nitwit and fall for a charming groom. Instead, she stood and reached out her hand. "Come, I shall help you up."

He threw her a wry smile but clasped her hand and stood. They had never been so close before, not while standing, at least. The extent of his height made her stature seem small and delicate.

Her mouth dried at the sight of him, so strong and tall, a man who was one of few who made her feel like the delicate flower she certainly was not.

"Thank you, Lady Anwen." His deep voice thrummed through her blood, and she reveled in the sound. One day he would use such a gravelly, alluring voice on the woman he chose to spend the rest of his life with. Anwen inwardly sighed; what a fortunate woman to listen to such a melody daily.

She walked about him, inspecting his person. "You do not appear injured," she said, dusting off his shoulders, which sported large clumps of mud. The moment her fingers touched his body, she knew she had made another colossal mistake. She snatched her hand away, cursing herself a fool.

What was wrong with her that she could not stop being so tactile with him? No matter how innocent the interaction, should anyone come across them, a scandal would ensue. Touching a man covered in mud indeed. Anyone would believe she had been rolling about with him on the ground.

Before she could say or do anything else inappropriate, Anwen returned to her horse and climbed back onto the saddle. Her skin burned, and she had the terrible notion that Mr. Clarence was watching her, wondering what had just transpired between them.

She shook the uncomfortable thought aside that he

would read into her care of him and her demands more than he ought. She was a viscount's sister. She would be concerned for anyone who fell off their horse before her. Mr. Clarence was not anyone special.

Liar...

The sound of Mr. Clarence soothing his mount caught her attention, and she turned to see him walk his horse through a nearby gate, before mounting himself.

Even with a horse with hands high as hers, he made mounting appear effortless. Lord Orford was fortunate to have such a competent groom.

"Well, I must be off, Mr. Clarence. I do hope you did not sustain any lingering injuries from your fall," she said, the need to flee him riding her hard.

He chuckled, walking his mount beside hers. "I did not, Lady Anwen. I shall be perfectly well."

"Very good then. Good day to you," she said, a little too formal and lofty for her liking, but she needed him to know that she was a lady, a woman of nobility, and while they could be friends, they could be nothing more than that.

He reached out and clasped her arm, pulling her to a stop before she could move away.

"Tomorrow, Lady Anwen? Mayhap I can show you around Lord Orford's estate if you're free."

"I'm not engaged," she blurted before she could think better of her words and decline his invitation. She really ought to wait for the marquess to invite her to visit and ride about his grounds, but surely if no one knew, what harm could there be?

The idea of spending another pleasant afternoon on horseback with a competent rider and amusing host was too much to ignore. There was nothing between them but friendship. She was being foolish to imagine feelings or reactions that simply were not there.

You need to stop lying to yourself, Anwen, and decline the invitation instead...

"Excellent, Lady Anwen. I shall meet you here if you prefer. As you stated, this field leads to the one that abuts Lord Orford's property line, and we can commence our ride then."

She nodded, rounding her horse and pushing her into a canter. She jumped the hedge grove that only minutes before Mr. Clarence had been thrown over, a smile tilting her lips.

"Now you're just showing off," she heard Mr. Clarence call out from behind.

She laughed.

The following morning Daniel woke early and bathed, certain there was still mud, and who knew what muck still in his hair. He stood before his looking glass, watching as his valet helped him into his riding attire.

Or better yet, the attire that made him appear his lordship's groom. The idea that Lady Anwen had no idea who he was tickled a part of his mischievous soul.

He really ought to tell her, of course. But she was so open around him, joyous and playful. To see her perhaps change into a quietly spoken, polite, husband-hunting woman like so many were in London would be a tragedy indeed.

But he knew he could not keep up this pretense for long. Eventually, she would find out who he was and, with that, his reputation. A man who did not seek a wife and had vices from the past that would terrify a virginal miss and send her running for the hills.

"That will be all. Thank you, John," he dismissed his valet, having had enough of the young man's attempts to polish his attire more than was necessary. He needed to look the part of a groom, not a lord pretending to be a servant.

He left his apartments, making his way through the house. The once-grand estate was in a terrible disrepair. Wallpaper was coiling off the walls, and the roof leaked in several places, causing rot to tarnish plastered walls, floor-boards, and joists.

The house would crumble in a matter of years if he did not commence repairs. At least now, as the marquess, he could start to fill the family coffers, his new steward more than capable of helping him turn the financial neglect around.

A rich wife would also help.

He dismissed the thought, even when the image of Lady Anwen floated before his mind's eye. She would be the perfect heiress to warm his bed. He liked her more than anyone he had encountered, and she was a local. She would know most of the villages and tenants that worked both her brother's estate and his. She would be an asset that he would not have to introduce to the area or help step into the role of marchioness. A lady of her breeding would have long been taught how to run one's own household.

Not that he was thinking of marrying anyone. Today was for riding through his estate with his guest. Nothing more.

He did not stop to break his fast but instead strode out the front door of his home and started for the stables, pleased to see that his horse stood out the front of the building, a groom holding him in wait for his arrival.

Daniel's eye slid over the rundown state of his stables, those too needing as much repair as the house, and he knew he must act.

He would send out word tomorrow first thing for repairs to commence. He had been here but a fortnight. It was time to act and not sit on these issues like his distant relative had.

"Your horse, Lord Orford. He's a little on edge this morning. I've lunged him, but be aware he's looking for a run."

"Thank you for the warning." Daniel hoisted himself up into the saddle, and before he could get his foot in the stirrup, his horse started forward.

"I see what you mean," he called out to his groom before reining in his horse's eagerness. Perhaps his mount was as eager to see Lady Anwen again as he was.

His thoughts rarely shifted to anything else since he first met her, and that in itself was telling or concerning. He wasn't sure which.

CHAPTER
SIX

I t took Anwen only a short time to make the ridge where she had agreed to meet Mr. Clarence. She sat atop her mare, looking down at the Orford estate. Again, she could see the sprinkling of workers going about their daily chores, but no sign of the elusive marquess.

She pursed her lips, adjusted her seat, and wondered what his lordship looked like. Mr. Clarence had not gifted her much of a picture when she asked it of him, merely his character, but she wanted to know much more than that.

Not because she was interested in knowing the gentleman but merely because she was nosy and enjoyed a little gossip with her sister every now and then. No doubt, with her sister's next letter, she would ask what was new in Surrey, and she wanted more than to tell her the new marquess was in residence and that he was a hermit like the late one.

The sound of cantering hooves floated through the air, and she turned to watch Mr. Clarence sprint toward her, a pleasant smile on his handsome face.

Her heart skipped a beat, and she schooled her features,

not needing him to know that in all her time at home, he was what occupied her thoughts the most.

More than what her family was doing in London or how many suitors her sister had, which would be many, she had little doubt. Instead, her thoughts were consumed with what Mr. Clarence was up to. Was he working hard on the estate, exercising the horses, and tending to their every need? Did the marquess seek him out regarding his horses? Did he get along well with the late lord's staff at Orford House? Was there a maid who had caught his attention?

The idea that he had a sweetheart made her heart seize. She did not want to think about things that should not concern her. It would be good if he were to be courting a woman of his rank. He could certainly not court Anwen, no matter how well they got along.

He was not of her world, the tragedy that situation was.

"Good morning, Lady Anwen," he said cheerfully, his smile warming her blood.

Anwen fought not to appear too eager, but never had she ever felt like she did around Mr. Clarence. The idea that she would soon go off to town and be courted by men she did not trust or care to know was a sobering thought.

If only she could be allowed to love and marry whomever she wished. Not that she was committing herself to feel more than a friendship for Mr. Clarence, but the choice seemed to have been taken from her merely because of the family she had been born into.

Very unfair, to be honest.

About to reply to Mr. Clarence, she heard a male voice call, "Lady Anwen." Anwen turned and found her brother's head groom cantering toward her from the direction of her home.

Fear settled in her belly, and she glanced at Mr.

Clarence. Being caught with a man, unchaperoned, was not in her plans for the day.

"Excuse me, Mr. Clarence. I must speak to my groom." She walked her mount over to where her servant sat on horseback, his attention flicking to Mr. Clarence curiously before meeting hers.

"What is it, Josh?" she asked.

"It's your brother, Lady Anwen. Word arrived this morning that he's to arrive tomorrow to take you to London."

"And you thought to ride out and tell me this?" Her tone held a little censure. Had her brother's servants been spying on her? Was that why her brother was returning without a word to her about it in his last communication?

She swallowed, not wishing to argue with her sibling, nor did she want to travel to London. How utterly boring her time there would be.

"Your maid sent word to the stables to inform you. She is packing as we speak and wanted to ask if you wish anything in particular sent to London."

Her servant's gaze moved to Mr. Clarence again, and Anwen understood why her maid had sent the groom out to speak to her. Someone at home knew of her outings and who she had been meeting these past few days and wanted to limit her time with Mr. Clarence before her brother's arrival. Not that the few hours they would keep her from seeing Mr. Clarence would lessen her brother's ire if he were already aware of her riding excursions with the neighboring estate's groom.

"I will return home directly and speak to my maid. Go on without me. I shall not be long."

Anwen waited until the groom was out of sight through the copse of trees before walking her horse beside Mr.

Clarence. "Alas, it would seem we shall have to bid each other goodbye. My brother is returning home to escort me to London."

A pained expression crossed Mr. Clarence's features before he took a deep breath and smiled. "A shame for us both, I think. I enjoyed our rides together. I had hoped I could persuade you to one more adventure."

"Adventure?" she asked, curious and forgetting all about leaving for London. An adventure with Mr. Clarence sounded heavenly, and could be her last taste of freedom before the shackles of marriage to an uptight, lofty lord shadowed her future.

"The late Lord Orford seemed to be an enthusiast of astronomy, and in the hunting lodge, which also acts as an observatory, there is a telescope. We encountered it when riding the estate and checking all the outbuildings and tenant housing that require work. The hunting lodge, however, seems to have been used frequently and is in good condition. Perfect for star gazing."

She could not meet Mr. Clarence at night, alone to watch the stars. How scandalous of her, but then, as he held her gaze, his beseeching blue eyes beckoned her to do something, anything she should not.

"I thank you for the invitation. Star gazing is not something that I have ever ventured to do before, but I cannot. It would not be proper to attend, and I must decline. I'm sorry," she said, commonsense prevailing for the first time.

A slight frown of disappointment settled between his brows. "If you snuck out, I could collect you on my horse. No servants or your brother need ever know." He paused, his dark blue gaze brooking no argument. "I promise I shall play the gentleman. I do not ask you to join me out of nefarious means. I merely wish to spend time with you."

Oh, how lovely he was, and how tempting.

However could she say no to such an invitation? And he was right. This evening would be the last time they could spend time together. Today would no longer be transpiring due to needing to return home to prepare for her brother's arrival.

She met Mr. Clarence's eyes and could not look away, and with that realization knew she could also not refuse.

"Very well, Mr. Clarence. I should love to star gaze with you this evening. But you must wait for me in the trees near the lake at the back of the gardens at my brother's estate. There is a large oak that tumbled in the last storm. I shall be there."

"Shall we agree to meet at midnight?" he asked, that small, playful smile back on his lips. Was he pleased she would join him? The eagerness in his eyes indeed indicated so.

"Midnight it is," she agreed. "But I cannot stay out long. My brother will undoubtedly arrive early. I should imagine he would have stayed at the Bells Inn this evening and will cover the last few miles at breaking dawn."

"I will have you home before you're missed, Lady Anwen." He tipped his cap and smiled, this time in no way hiding his pleasure. "Until we meet again."

She nodded and sighed when he turned his mount about and rode down the hill toward Lord Orford's estate. How was it that a groom was so utterly charming? So handsome that it ought to be not so. Perhaps it was fortunate that the late Lord Orford had no daughters, for no doubt they, too, like herself, would be all fluttery and not one's self around his lordship's groom.

Anwen turned and urged her horse toward home. At

least she had this evening to enjoy. One last night in Surrey with her friend before her future was set to begin.

When she had been in London last, she had not enjoyed her time, not like her sister. The men were all the same, paper cutouts of who was suitable and most accomplished in uttering sweet nothings that meant the same.

Her memory moved to Mr. Kane and his treatment, the falsehoods he had spewed that eventuated in him offering for another. How she had acted the fool during her first year in town, but never again. His treatment of her during the 1814 Season still sent shame washing through her at her naiveness.

She did not want to marry a man who lied and promised sweet nothings.

She wanted love. A partner. A friend. A man she could trust, no matter his rank.

SEVEN

Anwen kicked her heels near the fallen tree, her heart still pounding hard and fast in her chest after her attempt to sneak out without detection almost came to an abrupt halt.

At this late hour, she had expected all the staff to be abed, but it would seem not the case in her brother's home, and not this night. Only one solitary footman checking all the candles had been snuffed had still been lurking about.

She pulled her shawl closer about her, the chill in the air growing ever more pronounced the longer she stood there waiting for Mr. Clarence.

You should not be here, Anwen. Turn about and go home.

Still, she did not move, merely kept to the shadows and waited to see if Mr. Clarence would come and collect her as agreed.

The sound of horse hooves in the woods pulled her gaze toward the line of trees, shadowed and eerie in the dead of night before Mr. Clarence materialized in the moonlight.

This evening Mr. Clarence wore a great long coat buttoned up to his chin and a hat firmly placed on his head, keeping him warm. He appeared mysterious and deadly handsome. A thief in the night come to steal her away.

If only that were true...

"Good evening, Lady Anwen," he murmured, his tone deep and beckoning her to do what she should not.

She closed her eyes momentarily, fought not to be tempted more than she was before her fingers closed about his outstretched hand, and he pulled her up behind him on the horse.

"Hold on to me. We should be at the hunting lodge within fifteen minutes or so, no more, I should think."

"Very good," she said, steeling herself to wrap her arms about his waist. An odd sensation coursed through her when her fingers met around his stomach, linking and holding herself against him so she would not fall. He turned the horse around and cantered from the fallen oak, heading away from her home.

Anwen swallowed the nerves that fluttered in her belly. Her mind reeled at what she was doing and who she was with. He was a groom, a man she barely knew, but oh, how she enjoyed doing all the things she was not supposed to do as the well-bred young lady she was brought up to be.

He pulled and tempted a side of her that wanted to be free, live, and enjoy life. Not follow the rules, and marry a boring, pompous lord. Men who lied and just wanted a wife to have babies while they enjoyed their mistress's bed more than their marriage one.

Her chest pressed against his back, and the breath in her lungs seized when his gloved hand covered hers, pressing her hold into his chiseled abdomen. Anwen swallowed, glad Mr. Clarence could not see the burn of a blush that stole across her cheeks.

The contact between them felt intimate, something like

a husband and wife would do or a couple courting. Not two friends, one a lady, the other a groom.

Her fingers curled into the woolen material of his great-coat, his hand adjusting to her new hold. Anwen laid her head against his back, breathing deep the intoxicating scent of sandalwood and leather, two fragrances that meshed perfectly and were now her favorite for all time.

Just as you two go perfectly together.

Anwen pushed the thought aside. It was unhelpful to think in such a way. Nothing could come from their friendship.

Before long, the horse slowed to a walk and entered a clearing within dense woodland. Anwen spied the hunting lodge, the windows a beacon of bright light and warmth in the eerie forest.

"How delightful the lodge is," she said, sliding from the horse when he pulled to a stop. Mr. Clarence joined her, throwing the reins over the horse's head. "Go inside, Lady Anwen. I shall join you shortly. I merely need to settle the horse in a nearby stall."

Anwen did as he bade and entered the rectangular-shaped building that looked as welcoming as hers. A fire burned high and robust in the grate. Several candles were lit about the room and in the wall sconces. She walked about, taking in the masculine space decorated in dark green and blue-striped linen furnishings. A vase of wild-flowers sat on the table, along with a basket.

She strode over to the table and peeked inside the basket, her mouth watering at the cheese and red wine. Was that for them? How did Mr. Clarence get such fare? He certainly had a way with the cook if Lord Orford's servant allowed him to take such food.

Maybe they're lovers...

No, she would not think like that. Not think of Mr. Clarence in any romantic light. To do so was no use to either of them.

"I hope you like red wine," he said as he came through the door, closing it and shuffling out of his greatcoat. He watched her, a broad smile across his mouth, as he waited for her reply.

He looked like a rugged highlander with his long, curled locks and cheeks that were rosy from their ride. Her gaze dipped to his body, where her hands had pressed against and held his firm stomach. His trews accentuated his muscular thighs, strong from years of working with horses.

Stop, Anwen.

She turned and pulled the wine from the basket. "I do enjoy red wine, Mr. Clarence, but how were you able to get your hands on such a beverage, not to mention the cheese?" she asked, wanting to move the conversation away from what was spinning about in her mind.

Like what he would taste like. Would he be as sweet as the wine they would drink?

Not that she had ever kissed a man before, but the thought of kissing Mr. Clarence wasn't so awful as to dismiss.

"The cook loves me at Orford House. It did not take much to persuade her to give me what I needed. The wine and cheese were for a good reason."

"I hope you did not tell her the reason was me," she interjected, ignoring that his speaking of the cook and persuading her to whatever whims took his fancy sent a bout of annoyance and ill humor through her soul.

Maybe they *were* lovers?

"Perhaps you should have the cook here instead of me. Seems a waste since she's already half in love with you if she gives you such vintages to drink." She clasped two glasses, ignoring Mr. Clarence's silence at her jibe.

She heard his footsteps come up behind her and stop but a breath from her back. "Do I detect a note of jealousy, Lady Anwen?" he asked, clicking his tongue in disapproval.

"Of course not." She rounded on him and regretted the action the instant she realized he was far closer to her person than she first thought. He towered over her, his disheveled appearance calling to a part of her that did not want a perfectly combed and pressed husband.

She fisted her hands at her sides, glad he could at least not read her mind. "What an absurd thing to suggest," she replied in the haughtiest voice she could muster.

His amused grin did little to persuade her that he thought any different from what she said. "The chef at the Orford estate is a man, just to clarify. So unless I've become a molly since meeting you last, my interests do not lie with him."

Anwen felt her mouth gape, and not for anything could she form words.

"You were pouring wine, Lady Anwen?" he continued. "Or do you need my assistance?" He raised one brow, his attention moving to the glasses.

Anwen inwardly sighed and turned to pour the drinks as he suggested. Probably best, since having him so near discombobulated her to the point where she could not think straight. Determined to change the subject, she gestured to the room. "Is there not some telescope we're supposed to be looking through to see the stars?" she asked.

"It's in a room just behind this one. The room has no windows and barely a roof. A very clever design, I must say."

The idea held merit and made her even more curious

about what they were doing here. "I've never looked at the stars, other than with my own eyes."

"I'm the same," he admitted. "But when I came across this telescope, I knew I must take the opportunity if one ever arose to use it."

"Does Lord Orford not mind that you're using his property?" The thought of the marquess bursting in on them here, alone, eating cheese and drinking wine and using his telescope, was not something she wished to explain to her brother.

Who she would see in a matter of hours, more the pity.

"What he does not know will not hurt his lordship. Now, come," he said, striding across the room to a door to one side of the mantel. "The telescope is in here."

Anwen picked up their glasses of wine and followed him. True to his description, the room was sparse of anything but a tall telescope. A circular hole was indeed in the roof, and no windows were present.

Mr. Clarence shut the door, and like magic, the stars seemed to illuminate more brightly than ever before.

No other light penetrated their view, marring it in any way, and never had she seen something so beautiful. "It is like another world," she breathed.

"Millions of them, I would think," he answered, his voice a husky whisper.

Her skin prickled in awareness, and she nodded.

"Would you like to see the moon, Lady Anwen?"

"Yes," she whispered, the word thankfully not giving her nerves away. "I would."

CHAPTER
EIGHT

A nwen had never seen the moon so clearly. The bright orb was indeed a constant in the night sky, but seeing it under the telescope's magnifying effect was extraordinary.

"There are craters on the moon. I would never have thought. In fact," she continued, thinking out loud. "I suppose I did not think much about what it would look like. A sandy and barren place was all that came to mind."

"It is quite remarkable, is it not?" Mr. Clarence said. "I will admit I have made use of this telescope prior to tonight and enjoy my solitude here."

Anwen could see why he would. What a magical dwelling this small, quaint observatory was. With no nearby buildings, no light or sound penetrated the small space except those of nature in the surrounding forest.

"I shall miss our outings, Mr. Clarence. Thank you for making the few days I have known you enjoyable." Anwen stepped away from the telescope and picked up her glass of wine, sitting on a nearby chair.

"So your brother does indeed arrive in the morning? He

stood in the center of the room where the moonlight settled on his broad shoulders, making him as clear to see as if he were standing in candlelight.

She sighed, knowing she would miss looking upon such handsomeness. "He does. It seems my ploy to stay in the country has failed, and I will be dragged off to London after all."

"Where you may marry," he said, a statement, not a question.

She ought not to answer. If she married or not was no one's business and indeed not Lord Orford's groom's interest, but still, even knowing the proper etiquette, she decided to answer anyway. "Where I shall marry, yes."

A muscle worked in his jaw, and he clasped the back of his neck, watching her. Anwen could not help but wonder what was going through his mind right at this moment.

Displeasure? Annoyance? Panic or even perhaps jealousy?

Everything that was going through hers.

She narrowed her eyes, not for the first time contemplating that mayhap it was Mr. Clarence who was jealous and not her as he had accused earlier.

At his silence, she had to ask, "Is something the matter, Mr. Clarence?"

He shook his head, but she could see the muscle in his jaw clenched at her question. He was covetous, just as she had been when thinking of him having a sweetheart at Lord Orford's estate. A pity for them both, for nothing could come of their avarice or their desire for a different future.

"Not at all," he answered finally, walking over to where the wine bottle sat and pouring himself a full glass. He drank it down, refilling it immediately.

Was the man wanting to get foxed? "You know you have

to take me home this evening. Do not get so far in your cups that we will get lost."

"Would that be so bad if we did?" he answered, not turning to look at her.

A warm feeling floated through her stomach, and she took a calming breath, needing to keep her wits about her, not lose them to sweet, beguiling words.

"I would be ruined, so yes, it would be unfortunate. I would lose my family and friends, and all because I took a night to gaze at the heavens. Would it not be ironic that you could look toward such beauty and crash to earth but hours later."

"I would not let you fall, Anwen."

She met his eyes, forcing herself not to swoon into his strong arms and tempting expression. Hearing her name on his lips eased a longing she did not know she had.

The man was dangerous to her clear-thinking mind and ability to stay sane and not do something foolish, like what she wished, and fall to earth, preferably with him breaking her fall. "That is very gallant of you, but not a risk I'm willing to take." She paused. "And you should not call me Anwen. I have not given you leave." Devil take her, even though the thought of doing what he hinted was like an elixir that tempted the soul to live dangerously, throw everything aside, and grasp what she truly wanted.

A life outside Society. A marriage founded on friendship and love. Whether Mr. Clarence was that man was another possibility to ponder later, but he certainly drew her more than any gentleman ever had in London.

"A pity on both points," he said, turning and leaning against the sideboard. "I shall miss you, Lady Anwen." Now back to using her title, placing distance between them as he should. Just as she asked.

Even if that fact thinned her patience even more.

D aniel fought the urge to stride across the small room, clasp Lady Anwen by the shoulders, wrench her against him, and kiss the chit senseless. A good, long taste of her would satisfy his unabating craving and, with any luck, knock a little of her decorum aside.

Her eyes shone with a need that matched his, but he did not want to frighten her. He wanted her to come to him, to kiss him, before she left for London of her own fruition.

He had asked himself these past days why having her step forward and show him that she desired him was necessary, and it came down to the fact that if she did reach for him, she was kissing Mr. Clarence. A servant, a lowly groom, a man with very little to offer.

Not the marquess that he was. A man with a title, a seat in the House of Lords, more money than he knew what to do with, land, and a sprawling estate, as rundown as it was right now.

Should she kiss him, he would know she was not looking for a good match to prosper her family and their connections, but to have a genuine tie to one's partner in life.

A prospect that was hard for him to wrap his mind around. Not even his parents showed interest in him, even when it became clear he would inherit the title of Marquess of Orford, so consumed in their world, likes, and lives to bother with him.

But marriage? He was only seven and twenty. He had not planned on marrying anytime soon, if at all, preferring to stay in the country to live a solitary life.

Lady Anwen narrowed her eyes at him. "You're trying to

bait me to act foolish. Was that what you planned when you brought me here this evening, Mr. Clarence? I thought I could trust you. I thought we were friends."

Oh no, this would never do. He did not want her to think he brought her here for nefarious reasons. Certainly, they were not the only reasons, but he would not have denied her had she clasped his jaw, reached up, and kissed him. No man worth the title of gentleman would deny a lady.

And certainly not the man he once was, who enjoyed nothing more than a quick fuck.

He chucked, holding his hands up in surrender. "Truly, I did not. I wanted you to see the stars and the moon, that is all. I do not believe I have tried anything that would warrant censure from you. But I will state that, as for you, I cannot alter whatever thoughts are going through your mind, scandalous or not."

Her cheeks blossomed a rosy color, and she exhaled an indigent huff. Possibly without thinking, she strode over to him, standing nose to nose. "I know this game you're playing, Mr. Clarence, and you ought to be ashamed of yourself. I will not be baited to kiss you."

"Oh, ho ho," he said, chuckling. "I do not believe I mentioned kissing, but if that is what you're thinking, I'm more than happy to oblige." He ran a finger down her button nose, over the sweet groove above her tempting, succulent lips.

Lady Anwen's eyes widened, and like a punch to his gut, Daniel stilled. To touch her, tempt her to do wicked things with him was one thing, but to feel her soft lips that he ached to taste was not what he ought to have done.

Somehow in his teasing, he had also entrapped himself

into a situation where he could not let her leave without tasting her, if only once.

They moved at the same time. Their lips met and held but a heartbeat before she opened like a flower.

The heavens were indeed on earth this night.

She sighed, and he swallowed her need, deepening the kiss, recklessly clutching her to him and showing her what it could be like between a man and a woman.

She tasted of red wine, but sweeter, more intoxicating to his soul. Her hands fisted into his hair, and somehow, the kiss changed, became desperate, hard, and commanding.

Daniel fought for composure to keep his head, but he could not.

This kiss severed him at the knees, and the word trouble reverberated in his mind. He could not let her leave for London, and he certainly could not let this sweet Siren marry some faceless dandy.

He would have to follow if she left for town, and he knew what would ensue. Vices—not of the female kind—he had fought to remove himself from would tempt him once again, and then the truth would come out about his character. About who he really was, and she would never forgive his deception.

But he could not think about that right now. Not when Anwen was in his arms and kissing him senseless.

CHAPTER
NINE

Anwen did not know how it came to be that she was kissing Mr. Clarence, nor could she stop. He tasted of sin and red wine, two intoxicating elements she wanted to get foxed on and indulge in.

His large, strong hands clasped her hips, his fingers flexing through her riding ensemble. His touch sent heat to pool at her core, and she squeezed her legs together, trying to soothe the ache he caused.

"You're so beautiful, Anwen," he whispered against her lips, kissing the underside of her jaw and down her throat. A shiver stole over her body, and she clutched at his coarse shirt, trying to steady her legs, secure her thoughts, but there was no point.

She was utterly lost.

Merrily kissing her way to ruin. "We should not be doing this." This night, their familiarity, everything she had allowed to pass these last days was an error, but nor could she stop.

She fisted the linen in her hands, pulling him close. He did not deny her, submitted to her neediness, as eager as she. His mouth crashed down on hers again, and everything was perfect indeed.

The feel of his tongue, odd at first, soon lured her to enjoy the wonderful sensation. Her stomach clenched, and she moaned, unsure where the guttural, needy sound came from.

From wanting Mr. Clarence, Anwen.

"I do not even know your given name," she breathed, breaking the kiss to meet his eyes.

"Daniel. My name is Daniel." He kissed her again, and she wrapped her arms around his shoulders. Her breasts pressed against his chest, and she was sure she could feel the drumbeat of his heart.

But there was more to what she could feel. Things that no unmarried lady ought to recognize, and although she was very innocent when it came to the intimacies between a man and woman, she was not entirely void of knowledge of a man's anatomy.

The hardness in his trousers pressed against her stomach. Her head spun, and her lungs seized to gain air. She wanted to know more about him. What else could they do other than kissing that would have such an effect on him?

He broke the kiss, meeting her eyes. "Will you give me leave to call you Anwen? I think us kissing ought to grant me that one favor. After all, we're friends who share confidences, and now much more than that."

She nodded, wanting to hear him speak her name again. Thankfully she did not have to wait long.

"I want to eat you alive, Anwen. I want to do so many things with you."

The idea of leaving Surrey, this intoxicating man, her friend...dampened her mood and brought her senses crashing back to earth.

Anwen pushed out of his hold, clasping her arms as if to stop herself from reaching out and seizing him yet again. "There is no point to what we're doing. You're a groom, and I'm a viscount's sister. We should not be partaking in such scandalous behavior. You would be without employment, and I would be ruined if we were found out."

"People can desire each other and be from different social spheres, Anwen. Not everything is black and white, as you've been brought up to believe."

"I do not think that, but my family has expectations for my future, and I cannot disappoint them. They would never recover if they knew I was kissing his lordship's groom in the middle of the night in Lord Orford's hunting lodge."

"A little dramatic, is it not?" he stated, frowning at her. "I think it's honorable that you look past social norms and see me for who I am beneath any employment title or status."

But it wasn't theatrical. Her sister and mama may react shocked and disappointed, but her brother would seek retribution.

"I should go." She started for the door, and he clasped her hand, pulling her to a stop.

"Do not leave. I do not wish for you to go."

The pleading in his blue eyes almost undid her resolve to act the lady she was brought up to be. *Almost.*

"I cannot stay. I'm sorry."

She heard his steps close on her heels. "I will take you home. The woods are not safe at night."

Anwen was glad of his escort, but all the way home, having to hold his waist, press against his body for warmth and to keep her seat was another agony she did not think to endure this evening.

He smelled so good too, a scent she would forever

52

associate with him, and deep down, she knew she would think of Daniel each time she came across it in her life. The groom who stole her heart under a moonlit night while she broke his in return.

D aniel tried to push away his doubts as he escorted Anwen home, but they would not relent. It did not surprise him that she stepped away, stopping the intimacy from growing stronger.

It was the story of his life. Anyone whom he cared for and loved never stayed for long. His parents were often absent, only having fits of fancy to show affection and interest in his life, health, and education before flouncing off to whatever sparkly tidbit they fancied more.

His upbringing certainly explained why he never sought heartfelt companionship.

Until Anwen...

He dismissed the thought. He should have brought his mistress to Surrey and kept her here with him. At least then, he would have someone to warm his bed and never have absurd thoughts that someone may care for him.

Anwen had shown promising signs that she was different from any women he had met before, but it was not to be. If he told her now who he was, he would despise her change of heart. Any interest she showed after such a conversation would only cement the fact she was indeed like most debutantes and seeking marriage to better them-selves and their families.

Even if she were one of the kindest women he had ever met. Few would kiss a man not fit to wipe her boots, but Anwen had.

He placed his hand over hers on his chest, not wanting

to let her go. Wishing he had not started such a charade, but also thankful that he did. A contradiction, he knew, but one he could not change now.

He urged his mount forward, unsure when they would meet again and how he would tell her the truth. He did not know her well enough to know how she would react to learning the truth of who he was, but something told him it would not be pleasing. What a muddle he had made for himself, more complicated than the vices that often over-took his life when living in London.

"I'm sorry, Daniel," she whispered against his back, the soft touch of her lips against his spine seizing him with need, with regret.

He shook his head, the truth of his life on the tip of his lips. "Anwen," he began, but stopped when the sight of the Astoridge estate loomed before them in the darkness. "You are home," he said instead, keeping his secrets locked away.

She did not let go of him straightaway, instead, her hold tightened a moment before she relented and slipped to the ground, standing beside his mount.

Her eyes glistened up at him in the moonlight, and he fought the urge to dismount and take her sweet lips.

"Goodnight, Daniel. I wish you nothing but the best."

He smiled at her and watched as she started for the house, not leaving for his estate until she was safely through the terrace doors.

Safely away from him as she should be. He was a complicated man who seemed to make his life more convo-luted by the day, one she did not need or deserve to be part of.

CHAPTER
TEN

A nwen woke late, bathed, and dressed in preparation for seeing her brother again after several weeks. In the past, she had always looked forward to seeing him, hearing any gossip he may have come across during his travels, but not today.

Today meant she would have to leave her home and travel to London. Unless, by some miracle, he decided she could stay in Surrey and attend next year's Season instead.

A highly doubtful materialization, but one could hope.

She sat in the window seat of her room, staring out over her brother's lands, and contemplated how she could continue to pretend to be unwell. She supposed she could use rouge on her cheeks and make herself appear flushed. And if she rubbed her nose enough, it would give the appearance of someone with a trifling cold. But then her brother may send for the doctor, which would never do. The doctor would see through her gimmick, and she would be done for.

A light knock sounded on her door. "You may enter," she called out, glancing at the clock on the mantel to see the time. She had not heard a carriage and did not think her brother would be here so soon. Luncheon at the earliest if he had indeed stayed at the Bells Inn.

"Lady Anwen, a missive has arrived for you from Lord Astoridge."

Her maid passed it to her. "Thank you, Mary." Her maid dipped into a curtsy and left. Anwen broke the wax seal and read the missive with growing excitement and relief.

Dearest Sister,

I must quickly scrawl this message to you, for I'm to return to London before finishing my journey home to collect you for the Season. Please do not be alarmed, your sister looks to have captured the attention of the Earl of Brassel, and I must return to town to meet with his lordship and read further into his intentions. All of which I hope are honorable.

This, of course, will mean a delay in bringing you up to town, but do not despair; you will have some weeks in London before the Season is over, alas, they may be the last of the days, but we shall still make the most of your time in town.

Yours affectionately,

Dom

Relief poured through her like a balm, and Anwen jumped from her seat and whirled about. Her brother was not coming to collect her after all?

"Yes!" she squealed, running over to her armoire and searching for a clean riding gown.

The realization that she would not be leaving Surrey, leaving her home, was a boon she had not thought to occur. She halted her rummaging through her closet at the thought of Mr. Clarence. She had told him they were not to be. Had pushed him away. Would he be pleased to learn she was not to depart? Or would he think her fickle should she seek him out yet again?

She frowned, pursing her lips. To continue her friendship with the groom was doomed to end badly, and yet, she could not stay away. Their kiss last evening made heat thrum low and delicious in her stomach. No, she could not stay away, even though it would be best if she did.

But then, how was she to notify him that she remained here? It was not as if she could march up to Lord Orford's estate and ask the marquess if she could call on his groom in the stables. Her only alternative would be to ride near Lord Orford's estate and hope she came across Mr. Clarence as she had the first time they met.

Oh, she hoped it might be soon. The thought of being wrapped in his arms once more was too strong to deny. To be kissed and hear whispered, sweet words of fancy.

Anwen rang for her maid and tapped her feet until Mary entered with a cup of tea and some toast since she had not yet broken her fast. Her maid spied the riding gown thrown over a nearby settee as she placed the breakfast tray on a small table before the fire. "You wish to ride this morning, Lady Anwen?"

"Yes, my brother is not collecting me after all. If you would help me dress, I shall go directly."

"You will eat something first?" Mary suggested. Her maid, an older woman who had never had children, was as protective as she was meddling of her and Kate.

"I promise I shall eat and finish my tea before leaving. I'm quite famished, actually." Which was peculiar, for before her brother's letter, the thought of food had made her stomach turn.

"Very good." Her maid picked up the riding gown and started preparing it on Anwen's bed for her to change into. As Anwen sat and ate her toast, spreading a good dose of strawberry jam on top and drinking down her tea, she untied the buttons on her dress as far as her fingers could reach.

"What time should we expect you back, Lady Anwen? Will you return for lunch or dinner?"

"I shall be home for dinner, no later, I would not imagine." Her maid finished helping her change, and she was soon, whip in hand, striding toward the stables.

It did not take the stable hands long to saddle up her mount, and she was soon ready to depart.

"Luna is a little feisty this morning, Lady Anwen. Do not let her have too much rein, or she may get away from you."

"Thank you, Josh. I shall heed your advice." With the help of her groom, she mounted her horse and turned in the direction of Lord Orford's estate.

She cantered out of the yard and along a deer path before following the river where she had met Mr. Clarence that first day.

Their friendship was like fate. A meeting of two minds that would not have otherwise met had she not picnicked.

Anwen smiled, breathing deep the rich, fresh morning

air that smelled of grass and dew. How she loved Surrey and how pretty the area was. How delightful her life here had been growing up. She never wished to leave, and the thought of going to London, marrying some faceless man, and moving away was enough to break her heart just thinking about it.

Having cantered enough to hopefully take a little of the fight out of her mount, she pulled Luna to a walk and strolled through the trees, watching the birds and listening to the rabbits and other small animals scatter about as she drew near and passed their woodland home.

She was getting close to Lord Orford's lands, and excitement thrummed through her. Would Daniel be out riding today? He had dropped her off quite early in the morning, thankfully before anyone at her home had been awake.

He would be up. No groom had the opportunity to sleep in unless it was his day off, if his lordship granted such a boon.

Thundering hooves caught her attention, and she stopped her mount. Was Daniel nearby? Was he too out riding and reliving their time together as she was? Wishing she had concluded things differently last evening?

Did he miss her and was coming to watch her carriage roll away? What was he thinking after their kiss? At least now that she was not traveling to London, she could find out.

A horse cantered in her direction along the same path, but she could not make out the rider. She narrowed her eyes and watched, not wanting to look too eager, just in case it was not Daniel.

Her fears eased when she recognized his handsome face and familiar mount he rode most days.

The moment he saw her, his eyes shone with pleasure and surprise.

She touched her stomach, soothing her excited nerves at seeing him again.

He grinned, a mischievous light in his eyes as he pulled his mount beside hers, shaking his head as if he could not believe what was before him. "What are you doing here? I thought you would be many miles gone by now."

She schooled her features and fought not to throw herself into his arms. Maybe even steal another kiss or two.

"My brother has been delayed and had to return to London. It does not appear that I will be in London for some time and will only have to endure the last few weeks of the Season."

His grin morphed into a smile, and he shifted his horse closer. "You know what that means, do you not, Anwen?" he asked.

She lost herself in his eyes, wanting to know more about what it would mean between them. "What does it mean, Daniel?" she asked, using his name as he invited her to do the day before.

His eyes darkened, and he clasped the back of her neck, pulling her but a breath from him. Her eyes dipped to his lips, and hunger thrummed through her like a wild beast.

"It means I get to change your mind about us, which will mean more kissing to sweeten my end of the bargain," he said before closing the space between them and covering her mouth with his.

CHAPTER
ELEVEN

Daniel could not believe that Anwen was before him, that he had her once more in his arms. He had been riding throughout the morning, longing to hear her voice, to see her pretty, smiling face, and for a moment when he had first spotted her, he thought he might be imagining her apparition out of yearning.

He did not want to think of why he was feeling the way he was with the woman in his arms, but at some point, he would have to face the truth that he cared for her.

More than anyone in his life, and that in itself made him nervous. He'd never considered meeting anyone who would make him want to pursue a future. Not that he could seek one as the groom he was pretending to be, and soon he would have to tell her the truth and see if she forgave him.

Just one of many he would have to convey should he wish for a future with the woman in his arms. Anwen may forgive him his lie regarding his true name, but the vices that he fought to keep in his past may not be so easily overlooked.

Her fingers gripped the lapels of his coat, and he was thankful she had not as yet noticed that his attire today was of much finer quality than his usual garb.

With any luck, she would not, especially if he kept her occupied with what they were doing right at this moment.

Her lips brushed and sought his, opening to the demands of his tongue. She suckled him, a quick learner, and heat shot to his groin, intense and relentless.

She would undo him with a touch. He could not imagine their pleasure if she trusted him fully.

But he could not do that to her. He could not push for more than what he received right now. She was a maid, Astoridge's sister. He could not disrespect her ever.

She leaned into him, seeking more of him, and he knew he could not keep kissing her this way. Not if he were to keep the promise to remain honorable. "Come," he said, breaking the kiss. "Sit before me, and we shall ride together."

She kicked her boot free of her stirrup and he clasped her hips, lifting her before his saddle. Anwen riding side saddle today worked in their favor, and she sat across his lap, her arm wrapping naturally about his waist as if they had known each other for years, not merely days.

"Better?" she asked him.

Oh yes, it was much better and a taste of what he wanted. Not that he would ask for more. The gentleman in him prohibited it, even if the rogue growled to be freed. She was not a doxy, a woman of the night, but a viscount's sister whom he could not pay and then be free of.

"I did not think I would see you." He did not want to repeat what she had said to him the night before, but it hung between them unsaid. "How long do you think before your brother comes to collect you?" he asked, wanting to spend as much time as possible with her.

"A week or two, I should think from what he wrote. My sister has caught the eye of a earl, and he needed to meet with him. I'm sure Kate is thrilled. She's wanted to be married and running her own household for some time now."

"And you're not like your sister?" He took the reins of her horse before urging his mount forward. Her arm tightened about him, and he seized the opportunity to hold her close.

"No, for it would mean I would leave Nettingvale, and I dread the day I will have to say goodbye to Surrey."

"Because your husband will not live locally?"

"Yes."

He frowned, not liking that a slight, worrying frown settled between her brows. Or that her eyes clouded with sadness. Anwen was a beautiful woman who ought to be happy, animated, and loved. Not married off merely because she was a viscount's sister and some lord needed a wife.

Not that he really ought to have such opinions since he was, in fact, a marquess and quite capable of marrying himself.

If you marry her, she would not have to leave...

Not that he had not thought of that possibility already. The scent of her perfume floated up to tease his senses, lemon blossoms, and almost sweet enough to eat.

Behave, Daniel...

"I hope Lord Orford does not ride today. I would hate for him to find us in such an inappropriate position." Her frown deepened. "Maybe I should return to my horse. I do not wish to have you fired. Whatever would I do with my days then?"

"He is not riding today, trust me. There is no reason for concern." He dipped his head and kissed her temple. "When you travel to London, maybe I can have the butler persuade the marquess to go to town also. We could meet there and ride in the park as we do now."

She smiled at him, and her sweet lips beckoned him to close the space between them. Would he ever gain control over his urges with this woman? Something told him he would not.

"How much fun we could have should you do so, but I know that will be unlikely. I heard two of my maids speaking about Lord Orford just this morning, and he seems to be as much a recluse as the previous marquess and does not leave the estate."

"And how would the maids know such things since they do not even work for m—" he cleared his throat, having almost said me. "Do not work for Lord Orford."

Thankfully Anwen did not seem to notice his slip of the tongue and continued with her tidbit of gossip. "Oh, well, they're stepping out with two footmen Lord Orford employs. All their courtship was approved between the late Lord Orford, and there is talk that they will marry this year."

"How lovely for them," he said, his mind racing as to which two footmen may be stepping out with Astoridge's maids. If that were so, this could mean he would have to speak to his staff and mention that his daily rides were strictly to remain no one else's business. And he rarely left the estate, that was true, but he did leave the house, so he was not a total recluse.

"One of the ladies is my chambermaid, and I'm very

happy for her. She deserves to have a happy life. She's a lovely young woman."

He pulled the horse to a stop when they came across the hunting lodge where they had met secretly the night before. "There is wine in the lodge if you would like to stop for a quick repast."

"I would indeed enjoy that."

They dismounted, and Daniel tied up the horses while Anwen went inside. He stepped into the dim room, so different from last evening when he had lit a fire and multiple sconces and candles to illuminate the space.

Still, he shut the door to find Anwen pouring them a wine each. She passed him a crystal glass and strolled around the space, inspecting the lodge better during the day. None of the furnishings were his choice, not that he disliked the masculine decor, but it could use a little updating.

She stopped near the daybed and leaned against the headboard. "I like this building. It has a lovely air about it, do you not think?"

He thought about her words but wasn't entirely persuaded. "A lot of rowdy, drunk hunters would have gathered here over time, maybe a rendezvous or two."

She waved his words aside. "Well, it has lovely air and pleasant memories for me, at least."

"Had you ever been here before last evening?" He frowned, coming toward her, not enjoying the punch to his gut that she may have been part of previous hunting parties, where men hunted for women just as much as they hunted for game.

"No, not at all, but my recollection of last night in this space will forever be a memory I'll cherish. My first kiss."

Her first kiss...

A statement that was as pleasing as Mozart's music to his ears. He reached for her, wanting her in his arms.

"The night will forever remain in my mind also, Anwen. I like that I was your first kiss, but I would like it even more if you did not run from me as you did. I do not want to stop whatever is happening between us, no matter how scary it may be. I want to be your first kiss and possibly your last."

Her mouth opened with a soft gasp, and he could see the longing in her eyes. "I want you to kiss me again, Daniel." He did not deny her request. He dipped his head and seized her lips, leaving her in no way confused by how she made him feel and what he wanted.

Her.

CHAPTER

TWELVE

The morning passed in a haze of delight, and Anwen did not want to leave the hunting lodge, nor think of returning to Nettingvale to be alone and without the company of Daniel, but he wanted to show her something on Lord Orford's estate, and she could not say no.

"It is just up ahead," he called over his shoulder.

She grinned, taking pleasure in watching him ride before her. A groom? A man so far beneath her that she ought to be ashamed, but she could not be. Never had she met such a kind, sweet soul as Daniel, and a viscount's sister or not, she could not help how he made her feel.

She needed to be brave enough to hold on to what she wanted and bedamned what anyone else thought.

He made her feel alive for the first time in her life. The air was sweeter to breathe, the trees in the parkland around them taller and more magnificent than she'd ever noticed. The animals more varied and plenty.

Life had become a little droll before she met him, but now, oh no, now it was quite the opposite.

"We have arrived," he announced, stopping.

Anwen frowned and pulled her horse to a stop, over-looking a large lake she had never seen before. "Why did I not know this existed here on the Orford estate? I've lived here my entire life and have never heard anyone speak of it." She dismounted, leaving her horse to graze, and walked to the bank where a small, wooden jetty jutted out over the water.

"The previous marquess must have built it, I imagine. Maybe they used the lake when they were children to swim during summer."

"It is summer now." She met his gaze and saw the eagerness in his blue eyes. "And a very warm day, and we've been riding. Perhaps we ought to go for a swim."

"Can you swim?" he asked, reaching for his cap and throwing it onto the grass at their feet. Daniel soon kicked off his boots and sat, pulling the stockings from his legs.

"I was only teasing, Daniel. We cannot swim here together." Anwen glanced out over the lake, the idea growing in temptation, but could she be so bold?

Could she?

"Only if you can swim, of course," he stated.

She kicked off her boots and sat beside him, removing her stockings, not prepared to be the only one sitting on the side of the lake while Daniel had all the fun in the water.

"I can swim perfectly well, I will have you know. Not that I should swim, certainly not with a man who is not my husband, but..." She glanced around them and could not see anyone who would tattle to her family or Lord Orford that they had taken such liberties with his lake. "The day is terribly warm, and a swim will be refreshing after our morning ride."

"Very refreshing indeed," he purred, the deep timbre of

his voice making her heart skip a beat. "I did not think that you would join me."

Daniel closed the space between them, his large hand clasped her nape, and he pulled her in for a kiss. Anwen melted at the feel of him, his soft lips beckoning her to be bold and wild. She opened for him, deepening the kiss, and lost herself in his arms.

He pulled back, meeting her eyes, and she could see he was fighting the desire that rumbled inside her too. "You're unlike anyone I've ever known. A woman who is kind, not high in the instep, and willing to be friends with people that perhaps she should not be."

She clasped his cheek, not favoring his disregard for himself in such a way. "I will admit that when we first met, I tried to remain aloof and, shamefully, keep my social status a well-known entity between us, but I could not for long. You are different from anyone I've ever met too."

"Even the other gentlemen you were introduced to in London?"

Anwen scoffed and thought back to her first Season and what a disaster that had been for both her and her sister. "I enjoyed London; at least, that is what I allowed my brother to believe. But in truth, I was happy to return home. Kate loves London. I do not. While Hyde Park is enjoyable to promenade and Rotten Row is a worthy place to ride, it is not home. Not these magnificent parklands."

Not to mention Mr. Kane lived in London with his new wife, the fickle gentleman whom she couldn't help but compare all other gentlemen against, giving none of them a good character reference.

"That is very true." Daniel pulled at his shirt, freeing it from his trousers, and ripped it off over his head, laying it on top of his stockings.

Anwen felt her mouth dry at the sight of his chest. She bit her lip, knew she ought to look away, to take in anything but the man beside her, but she could not. Her eyes would not shift from his chiseled abdomen or the sprinkling of hair on his chest.

Without thought, she reached out and touched him there. The coarse hair tickled her palms as she ran her hand over his person.

"No gentlemen courted you when you were in town?" he asked, his voice hoarse.

"Oh, they did, and maybe even at one time I was hopeful he would ask for my hand. But it was not to be," she answered, unable to stop touching him and not wanting to talk about the popinjay Mr. Kane.

"His failure to win you is my fortune." His eyes watched her keenly, seemingly oblivious that she found it terribly hard to think of anything at all, and certainly, her time in London when his heart beat hard against her palm, his warmth warming her skin.

"Or he was after a fortune, which I did not have at the time."

He reached out and took her hand, playing with her fingers. "You're the daughter of a viscount. I should imagine you have fortune enough to satisfy any man."

She thought about his words and then decided there was no harm in telling him the truth. "My brother almost lost the estate before marrying Paris. With her fortune, she saved our family, or at least our home and lands. From what I have learned, my brother needed to marry a woman of wealth. It was advantageous that he married Paris, who was both rich and the love of his life. Fortunate, was he not?"

. . .

"Very fortunate indeed." Daniel looked over the lake in thought. He had not known the Astoridge family had fallen on hard times. Did this mean her dowry was low? That she allowed a groom to court her, an impoverished man not worthy to kiss her boots, nevertheless her sweet lips, only made her more beautiful.

She could travel to London, marry a wealthy lord, and have a safe and easy life, and yet, she sat beside him, her neighbor's groom, kissing him, talking with him about all manner of things, a man not her equal.

But you are her equal. Tell her the truth, Daniel.

She pulled free from his hold and started undoing the buttons on her riding jacket. "You better finish getting undressed. We're to swim, are we not?"

Daniel swallowed hard and pushed down the rake in him that salivated at the thought of Anwen in nothing but her shift. How much could he withstand of her teasing? She tried his self-constraint daily, and he feared she would push his boundaries until they snapped.

She smiled at him, mischievous and with trust, and the panic rising through him that he would push her for more than she was willing to give eased. No, he would never hurt her or make her choose between propriety or him.

He fumbled with his attire, not wanting to be left behind.

The buttons gave way on her jacket, and he bit back a groan. The shirt beneath gaped, revealing an abundance of breasts. She slipped it over her head, pushing down her skirt, standing in nothing but her shift and stays, heedless of how she appeared before a man.

Especially a man of his ilk...

The stays too soon fell at their feet before she ran to the end of the dock and jumped, heedless, into the water.

Daniel ground his teeth, knowing the shift would be transparent wet. His attempts at gentlemanly behavior were already holding on by the skin of his teeth, and this would double his agony.

You will not seduce her, damn it.

With a fortifying breath, he followed her into the water and yelped the moment he surfaced. "Damn it, it's cold, Anwen! Mayhap, this is not a good idea."

She turned, running her hands along the top of the water. "Do not be a baby, Daniel. It's only water."

He supposed that was true, diving into the water again and cursing the cold while also enjoying the exhilarating knowledge of where he was and with whom.

THIRTEEN

Daniel came out of the water and reached for her. She tried to leap away, but he was too quick and pulled her against him.

"Where do you think you're trying to swim off to?" he whispered against her ear, sending a shiver down her spine that had nothing to do with the cold water they were ensconced in.

Her back, pressed hard against his chest, meant she could feel every breath and hard muscle against her. The sensation was slippery, sensual, and intoxicating all at once.

She closed her eyes, relishing his hands splayed across her stomach, holding her prisoner. Not that she was fighting to get away. What sane woman would want to swim away from such a man?

A groom, you mean...

She pushed the unhelpful, snobbish thought aside. He may be a groom, but he was her friend and perhaps much more than that. Although she was unsure exactly what was happening between them, she knew she did not want to stop seeing him.

Days such as the one they had enjoyed had been the best this summer, and nothing had come close to how much she did not want their time to end.

"Over there," she answered finally, gasping when his lips brushed the lobe of her ear. The man's ability for seduction, for temptation, was ridiculously good. Did he even know what he did to a woman and the responses one had when they were in his arms?

He certainly did not seem to care if he did.

"But I like you here. Tell me you like the feel of me too."

Heat and longing pooled at her core, and she clutched his arms to ground herself from his allure. "You know that I do. I would not allow you to hold me thus if I did not enjoy your touch," she admitted, turning her head to meet his eyes.

His wicked grin almost undid her resolve to remain chaste and good, everything a young woman of a good family ought to be. She should not be here, swimming with a groom of a neighboring estate and relishing every scandalous moment of it.

Her family would disown her should they ever discover what she had been up to. Even so, that was not enough for her to stop his hold on her. Halt his words of seduction and eyes that implored her to do what she desperately wanted.

Oh dear, she was going to hell for her thoughts...

He leaned forward and kissed her, and she turned, needing to taste him, kiss him without restraint. His hands wrenched her against him. With just a shift on, there was little to keep her from feeling his muscular, male body, so opposite to hers.

She sighed at the rough, hard planes. Without thought,

Anwen turned in his arms and slipped her legs about his waist, enjoying the heat that licked every inch of her form.

Her body was afire. Burning with a need that was unknown, but wonderful too. She ached in strange places, locations that wanted to be soothed and petted, stroked, and for reasons she did not understand.

This was madness. Yet, she could not stop tumbling toward this wonderful new sensual world he was introducing her to.

Her sex brushed something hard, and realization struck that she was not the only one affected by their kiss. A part of him, one that she never thought to know until her wedding night, pressed against her. She wore nothing beyond her shift, leaving very little between them.

His hands clasped her bottom, pressing her against his hardness, and she moaned. Sensation, thrilling and maddening, thrummed through her, and she rocked against him, heedless of where they were or what was happening. All she knew was she needed something that he could deliver.

"Anwen," he groaned, his voice husky with need but restraint. "I want you but will not have you like this."

She nodded, kissing him again. The time for talking about anything but what they were doing to each other was long gone. "What if I want you," she admitted, breaking the kiss long enough to utter those words.

A pained expression crossed his face, and a muscle worked in his jaw. "I can do other things that will keep you a maid."

She nodded, unsure of what she was agreeing to but knowing she would not survive if he did not do something, anything, before she combusted.

"I trust you, Daniel," she said, and the determination in his eyes sealed her fate.

Daniel was going to hell. He was playing with fire as much as he was playing with Anwen. But he could not stop. Could not halt rolling her hips against his cock and driving them both to the point of explosion.

And he would come. That was certain, even if she were unaware of what happened between a man and woman during such trysts. Her bottom fit perfectly in the palms of his hands. He wished he could see her tight globes, but little matter, her pebbled nipples pressed against her shift, giving him a sight he would not soon forget.

His mouth salivated to suckle them. The idea of laying her on the wooden deck and tasting her other sweet lips doubled his desire. Her cunny moved up and down his cock, so close to being one, so tantalizingly near he could almost taste fucking her.

"Daniel," she moaned, moving of her own accord, her body knowing instinctively what to do, even as innocent as she was.

"Have you ever felt like this before, Anwen?" He needed to know. Needed to hear that he was the first.

You will not be the last if you do not tell her the truth.

"Never," she breathed, murmuring incoherent words against his mouth as she kissed and undulated against him.

"Do you want me to tell you what is happening?"

"Yes." She bit her lip, her eyes heavy with desire.

He kissed her, deep and long, moved her, and almost lost control of himself. She felt so good, fit him to perfection. His body ached for release to glide into her wet cunny and sate himself in her heat.

"This happens between a man and woman who give each other pleasure. There is more, and you will see." Very soon, she would realize if he had his way.

"I want more, Daniel." Her raspy, breathless words called at a part of him, the dark, roguish side that took what he wanted and gave little in return. But he would not do that to Anwen. She was not some paid strumpet in an alleyway or a wife deprived of love and affection. This was a woman he wanted to please, to enjoy as much as she was relishing him.

Who knew that the art of giving would be so rewarding?

He thrust his cock along her heat, teasing the little nubbin that would catapult her into pleasure.

Her eyes widened, and she threw back her head, exposing the long lines of her neck. He kissed her there and held her tight as he labored against her, wanting her to shatter in his arms. To call out his name.

He glanced at the delicious sight of her breasts, visible through the wet shift. His stomach clenched, and his balls tightened. She was a Siren, a woman he had not thought to meet, certainly not in the wilds of Surrey, but here he was.

All but fucking his neighbor's sister while pretending to be a groom.

And she loved every fucking minute of it.

"I want to do so many things to you, Anwen. I want to drive my cock into your sweet, wet cunny and fill you, inflame you until you scream my name."

"Oh yes," she mewled, her feet tightening about his waist, pulling her closer to him.

"I want to lay you on a bed of silk sheets and run my tongue over every inch of your body. I want to suckle your quim, flick the sweet little bead that you do not even know exists. I want to see you sprawled on my bed, sated and well-fucked by me. I want everything." Daniel started at his words, unsure where that last declaration came from, but nor could he regret what he said. He did want her and everything that they could do together.

There was nothing wrong with desiring another who felt the same as you and acted on that desire. He had never been so vulnerable with another, but something told him he could trust Anwen.

"Daniel." She held him tight, and he knew she was about to come. Her fingers gripped his shoulders, her body pressed against his, rose and fell with each of their strokes. They made a beast with two backs, not an inch separating them.

"Enjoy, my darling," he said as he watched, entranced as the first of her pleasure ripped through her.

He had never felt more like a man or alive in his life.

FOURTEEN

L ike the stars she had seen in the night sky with Daniel, so too did she now see them on Earth. Her body pulsated with the most delicious feeling she had ever had come over her. Like her body was not her own, had kept a wicked and wonderful secret, and was only now giving her a glimpse into another reality she did not know existed.

Now privy to what she could have with Daniel, how he could make her feel, how would she ever remove herself from that? An impossibility, for even now, as she floated back to earth from wonderous heights, she thought of when she could see him again.

When they could meet and be alone, such as they were now.

She was a wicked woman, but how wonderful being tainted was.

He kissed along her neck, not the least eager to let her go. Warmth flowed through her veins, making her body lax and weak.

"You're so beautiful," he whispered into her ear, pulling a smile to her lips.

She chuckled when he nibbled on her lobe. "And you are very clever. I had no notion such a feeling could come over me after what we did. As a woman, I feel a little irritated that this secret has never been divulged to me before." She dipped her head and kissed the tip of his nose, marveling at how handsome he was and that he liked her.

He chuckled. "Well, I do not think it would be wise for the mamas of the *ton* to tell their charges of such possibilities. It would not be long for upstanding young ladies like yourself to revolt and no longer be so upstanding." Daniel wiggled his brows, and she couldn't help but laugh at his insight.

"You are possibly very right." He spun them in the water, and Anwen took a calming breath, wishing this happy day would never end. But she could not allow this feeling of complete contentedness to sweep her away. She was a viscount's sister, daughter to one too, and had obligations she could not shy away from.

No matter how much she wished she could. The thought of leaving Surrey and Daniel was abhorrent. How she would miss him and this carefree, darling time in her life.

"It will be challenging for me to go to London. I shall miss you even more now," she teased, grinning.

He clasped her waist and tickled her there. She yelped and fought to free herself, but alas, it was useless; he was too strong.

"Do not say such things. The thought of you departing covers the sun warming our skin and leaves a shadow."

She studied him momentarily, reaching up to wipe a

long lock of hair from his face. "So poetic. You are a man of many talents."

"Mmmm, you have no idea, Lady Anwen."

She pushed out of his arms at his use of her title and swam away. "Do not call me that. Here we are, just Anwen and Daniel. Two friends swimming together on this warm summer's day. Nothing more and nothing less than that."

"Ahh, but there is more than that between us, is there not?" he said, reaching for her outstretched leg and dragging her back to his side.

She wrapped her arms around his neck, playing with the damp curls on his nape. "As troublesome as it is for us, I do believe you're right. But it is not without its complications."

His face hardened at her answer before he clasped her face and pulled her in for a kiss. He plundered her mouth, leaving her reeling for purchase.

This was wrong. Terribly crass and the start of her ruin, and yet, she would not have it any other way.

Daniel soaked in a bath later that evening, the thought of Anwen never far from his mind. After today when he'd brought her to climax in the lake, he did not think he'd ever envision anything so beautiful again. The memory of her would fill his lascivious thoughts forever.

He wrapped his hand around his hard cock, and thought upon the moment, her rasping sighs, his name on her lips, her body as it rode his throughout her orgasm, giving her what she wanted while leaving her a maid.

He really needed some accolade for not fucking her. He

could have taken her, and she would have welcomed the intrusion, so lost was she in the moment's passion.

But he had never been that kind of rogue, no matter how debauched he had been in the past, and he would never stoop to such levels.

But damn it all to hell, if they continued with their interludes, how the hell was he going to keep himself from doing what he mustn't?

He stroked his cock, increasing the tension. The idea of having her in this room, her hand wrapped around his member, or perhaps her succulent mouth, was too much, and he shuddered his release. He sucked in a startled breath, the discharge long overdue.

This would never do; his craving for her was beyond his strength, and he needed to get a hold of himself. He reached for his drying cloth and stood, stepping free of the water.

Already his mind raced as to when he would see her again, what they would do and speak about. He would never sleep in this state. Throwing on a pair of buckskin trousers and riding boots, along with a clean shirt and jacket, he headed out the door, determined for repast at the local inn where he could drink his cravings into oblivion.

The journey into the small village did not take long, even when he had to rouse the stable hand to help saddle his horse. The village housed one inn, a church, a school, a blacksmith, and a very modest modiste who also acted as a tailor.

He pulled his horse before the inn and threw the reins at a willing stable boy, along with a silver coin to make his day.

The lad whooped, a broad smile on his lips at the unexpected boon. Daniel entered the lodging, glad to see all of those present did not know him as the new Marquess of

Orford and certainly would not guess due to the lowly condition of his clothing.

He sat at the bar, ordered a tankard of beer, and drank deep, letting the scent of sweat and alcohol bombard his senses. Busty barmaids came back and forth from the kitchens, carrying meals for those traveling through, some men taking the opportunity to pinch the barmaids' bottoms or breasts.

The women's cackling laughs and the men's salacious words echoed about the room. For the first time that evening, Daniel felt the strain of his thoughts relent. Watching the lower class around him enjoy their evening enabled him to melt away to be all but invisible. Giving him more time to think of his pretty neighbor and her sweet mouth.

Would he follow her to town if she were to leave for London? Inheriting the title of Marquess of Orford had saved him in many ways, forcing him to leave the city and all the vices that held so much power over him.

Sex, gambling, getting foxed, and repeating those vices daily.

As much as he enjoyed Anwen's company, being around all that he had fought to remove himself from, no longer craved, made his throat close in alarm.

"You're not from around ere, are ya?" a woman said at his side before she leaned against him, watching him as if he were a delicious sweet she wanted to lick. She was pretty, in a hardened kind of way her life had afforded her. A woman who knew how to take care of herself and his needs should he just say the word.

"No, I'm not," he answered, contemplating using the barmaid to release the pent-up desire that roared within him over Anwen. Emotionless rendezvous had suited him until he had met his neighbor. Anwen had him all at sixes and sevens, making him want things he'd never thought to need.

He ground his teeth, unsure what he ought to do.

"Care to come with me? You look like a man who needs a little female attention." She ran her hand over his arm, one finger sliding down to his wrist. "A little coinage between you and me, and you'll leave a lot happier than ya are now."

Daniel stood, downing the last of his beer. The young woman's eyes grew wide with expectation, and she flounced off, pulling him toward the back of the taproom.

They entered a dark room with one bed and a sconce burning low on the wall. The window had ripped drapes pulled closed on the night. His nose twitched at the stale, unpleasant scent coming from the room.

The woman lay on the bed, lifting her skirts and gifting him with a view he'd been desperate to see, but not from the woman before him.

His beer threatened to make another appearance, and he cringed. "My apologies, miss, but I have another appointment elsewhere. Good evening to you," he said, ignoring her words of dissatisfaction. He flicked two silver coins that landed on the bed, ceasing her moaning, and retired.

There was only one woman who could sate his desire, and it wasn't a tavern whore. Even if those women had been more than capable of scratching his itch in the past, they no longer sufficed.

A troubling fact he would need to address soon before he went mad.

CHAPTER

FIFTEEN

Anwen sat out on the terrace, the moon dropping lower in the night sky as the evening ticked slowly away. Even now, several hours after leaving Daniel, her body still trembled at the thought of him and what they had done.

The exquisite pleasure he had wrought upon her.

She puffed on a cheroot, one she had found in her brother's desk drawer, and thought of little else but a groom who had captured her heart and soul. How would she depart for London and leave him behind? How could she even contemplate marrying another when the thought of someone touching her, kissing her as Daniel had, had made her shiver in revulsion?

As if her reflection of him had made him morph before her, the apparition of him striding across the lawns of her house appeared.

He could not be here? Surely she was dreaming of him coming toward her, his long, muscular thighs eating up the space between them, his buckskin trousers pulling taut, hiding little from her imagination.

"Daniel?" she whispered, still uncertain she was not seeing a ghoul.

The wicked, knowing grin formed on his lips, and she stood, walking to the top of the terrace steps. "What are you doing here?" she whispered.

"I could not sleep," his deep baritone declared before standing on the steps. "I had to see you."

Warmth wrapped around her like a winter cloak. "That is very sweet of you, but it's late." She glanced back into the house, ensuring they were alone. "It would be past two in the morning, I'm certain."

"I did something this evening that I'm not proud of, but I needed to know something about myself that I've never realized before."

Anwen clasped her hands, and she was not entirely sure she wanted to know what Daniel had done to know his true self. Even so, she knew she would go mad if she did not find out what that was. "Enlighten me."

He took her hand and, glancing up at the house, dragged her into the shadows on the terrace. "I have not been myself since I met you. I cannot sleep or eat, nevertheless function as I should because you are all that occupies my mind. I know you should not, I'm not a worthy man, but I still cannot help how I feel."

Anwen held his hand firm, having never been so lovingly spoken to before, and certainly not from a man.

"I knew I would never sleep, so I left Orford House and traveled into the village for a beer at the inn. I ah..." He ran a hand through his hair, meeting her gaze before looking along the terrace.

She swallowed, not particularly liking where this story was headed, and yet, now, she had to let him finish. "What did you do, Daniel?" she asked.

"I thought that if I lay with a woman, I could ease the need I have for you with her body."

Anwen let go of his hand and frowned. Ease his need with another woman? "Are you trying to tell me that you were intimate with another woman because I would not give myself to you fully?" she asked, unable to hide the astonishment in her voice.

"I did think that, yes," he said, reaching for her again, which she avoided.

She stepped away from him, leaving him in the shadows. "I do not think you should have told me this, Daniel. You are not true."

"No, Anwen, listen. I went to the inn, and I thought about tupping some faceless woman, but when I realized that woman was not you, I could not. For the first time in my life, I did not slake my lust on a willing participant merely because of convenience. I care about you so much that I cannot think straight. You're the first woman who has ever niggled under my skin, and I like that you're there." He paused, holding her gaze and not looking away this time. "What I'm saying is that I care for you and that I do not want anyone else, but I need to know if you feel the same."

Relief poured through her that he had not been unfaithful. Without words, Anwen threw herself into his arms, taking his lips in a searing kiss. The kiss was deep, quick, and full of need. Their hands clung to each other, desperate not to let go.

"I only want you," she admitted. "I do not want to marry a rich lord or wealthy land owner. I want you."

He scooped her into his arms and carried her in through the terrace doors. Spying a daybed, he laid her down. Anwen shuffled up her gown, the need coursing through her like a rush of heat she wanted to wrap herself in forever.

He kneeled before her, her broad-shouldered, muscular groom, and tore at his footfalls. His cock sprang free, and Anwen gasped and bit her lip as he stroked his manhood before her.

"It's not what I imagined." She reached for him, running her finger over the tip of his shaft.

Daniel closed his eyes at her touch, and she could see he was fighting some unknown war within him.

"Tell me I can have you, Anwen. Please do not deny me now."

She grinned, reaching up to pull him down. He came willingly, taking her lips. She wrapped her legs around his waist and, reaching between them, guided him to her core. "I'm not going to deny you anything, Daniel."

"Oh God," he groaned, thrusting into her, making them one.

Anwen froze at the searing sting that assailed her. Daniel stilled, kissing her lips, nibbling her chin as he waited patiently.

"Tell me when you're ready," he breathed against her neck.

Taking a fortifying breath, Anwen fought to relax. This was natural. Couples did this kind of thing all the time. Surely it would not hurt so much the entire duration.

"I'm ready." She wiggled a little, and he pulled back before thrusting into her again. This time, there was no pain, just the odd, full sensation that felt satisfying.

He moved again, then similarly, and before Anwen could fathom what was happening, she was shifting with him, reaching, wrapping her legs about his hips, pulling him deeper, wanting him harder, faster.

"Anwen...dear God, you're going to be the end of me."

She wanted to be the end of him so that they could start

fresh together, just the two of them, forever. She clasped his face, watched him take her, fulfill her.

His eyes darkened in hunger and something else she could not name. What was he thinking? Something told her he felt as wonderful as she did but was there more to his dark, stormy eyes?

"You feel so good." She kissed him, thrusting her tongue against his, their mouths mimicking what other parts of their body were doing.

"I've wanted you so much. From the first moment I saw you, I wanted you."

His admission warmed her soul, and she nodded, knowing that deep down, he, too, had overtaken her mind and soul. How was she ever to travel to London now and leave him behind?

She could not. They would have to elope, leave Surrey together, and start a life far away from Lord Orford and her brother, who would never approve.

"I have thought of no one but you, too," she admitted, glad that there were no secrets between them.

He clasped her thigh, lifting her leg and taking her with relentless strokes. Anwen threw her head back, relishing the course of vigorous lovemaking.

She ached, her body thrumming with the sweet sense of another climax. "Yes, Daniel," she called out, throwing her head back as her body convulsed about his manhood. The sensation was similar to the one she had with him earlier that day, but also different.

This release was deeper, more fulfilling, and longer, making her feel closer to Daniel than she ever had.

He groaned, thrusting into her, heedless of where they were or who could come upon them at any moment. "I'm going to come," he rasped.

She clutched him to her, wanting him to join her in the exquisite dance of pleasure.

He swore against her neck and shuddered, his pulsating cock wringing the last of her orgasm.

After several minutes he collapsed at her side, their breathing ragged. Anwen could not wipe the silly grin from her lips. She looked up at Daniel and found him watching her, a look of awe on his face.

He rolled toward her, clasping her cheek in his hand. "What are we going to do, Lady Anwen?" he asked. "For I surely cannot let you go now."

She chuckled, wiggling into his arms, renewed need already sparking to life within her. "I have a plan, but I must think more about it. Shall we meet at the lake again this afternoon? I know you have work to do, but I can wait all day if necessary."

"I will be there. After lunch, we shall meet, for there are things that I, too, need to speak of."

She nodded, hoping that whatever he needed to say was nothing to jeopardize her plan for them to elope. In all truth, it was the only way. Her family otherwise would never approve.

CHAPTER
SIXTEEN

Anwen scrunched up and threw the missive from her brother, which had arrived this morning, to the floor. Still, her eyes stung and were itchy from lack of sleep, and being woken up early after her night of debauchery was not ideal.

Not that she could have slept for too much longer in any case. Not when she had an appointment to meet Daniel...

The thought of him brought a smile to her lips and butterflies to flutter in her belly. Remembering their time together after he had surprised her by calling on her in the middle of the night was a memory she would cherish for the rest of her life.

Hopefully, she would live and enjoy life with him if he agreed to elope with her.

After they were married, there was little her brother could do. They would consummate the marriage straightaway, and if her brother truly loved her, he would relent and give her the small dowry she was to inherit. Not that it was much, but it would be enough to keep them for some time before they gained employment.

Anwen pushed back the covers and went about her morning tribulations. She could work as a governess, a lady's maid, or even a companion until they decided to have children. Did Daniel want to have children? She supposed that was something else they should discuss.

She quickly dressed and had her maid set her hair, ordering the carriage.

"Are you going out, Lady Anwen?" her maid asked as she set the bonnet about her hair.

"Unfortunately, yes, and it will delay my ride this morning." And her rendezvous with Daniel, but she had to do what her brother asked, or he would wonder at it. "Lord Astoridge has asked me to call on our new neighbor, Lord Orford. Many years ago, they went to school with each other at Eton but lost contact. My brother wants me to welcome him to the county and invite him for dinner when the family is back in residence."

Her maid nodded, a small smile on her lips. "I'm certain Lord Orford will enjoy such a warm welcome from the family. Will you need a chaperone, Lady Anwen?"

"Yes, thank you, I will. You may attend me, but we shall not be too long, I would imagine, an hour at most."

"Yes, Lady Anwen." Her maid started for the door. "I shall collect my shawl and meet you downstairs, if there is nothing else you need from me."

"No, that will be all, thank you. I'll be down directly."

Anwen stood in front of her full-length mirror and checked her gown and bonnet. Today she appeared much different than her usual attire. Gone was the riding habit, and instead, she wore a light green carriage dress and morning jacket. The gown accentuated her small waist and other feminine parts that men particularly enjoyed staring at. She reached for a fichu and slipped it into the bodice of her gown, not wanting Lord Orford to get the wrong impression about her. She was, after all, a woman who would soon be married.

The carriage ride over to the Orford Estate was of short duration, and within fifteen minutes of leaving home, the carriage rolled through the gates to the marquess's front gardens.

The house was as impressive as theirs, except maybe in need of repairs here and there, which were much more noticeable when up close as she now was.

The carriage rolled to a stop before the house, and, doing the right thing, Anwen waited for Orford's footman to open the door and set down the steps. She took his offered hand and alighted, glancing about the yard. Her attention moved to where the stables sat, and she wondered if Daniel was within the stone walls, working hard tending the horses. She had come before their allotted time, so the possibility that she would see him made excitement thrum through her veins.

"This way, Lady Anwen," the footman said, escorting her toward the front door.

She glanced up at the house, four stories high and rectangular. The stonework on this estate was much more ornate than theirs, except two windows she could see from this angle had broken panes of glass.

Poor Lord Orford must have inherited a house that required work, possibly more than he thought to endure.

The home's foyer was much cleaner and without any obvious damage, and staff moved about the space, working and disappearing into rooms to finish their chores.

"If you would wait here, Lady Anwen." The footman moved over toward a room she assumed was where Lord Orford was situated, except already Anwen could hear male voices, loud and very much engaged in a heated conversation.

She frowned, turning to her maid, who followed close on her heels. "I shall not need a chaperone in the library. You may wait here on this chair," she said, moving toward the door.

The door stood ajar, and she waited beside it, wondering why one of the men's voices sounded familiar. She had not met Lord Orford before, not even when she was briefly in London the year her brother married Paris.

"What is it, Thomas?" she heard who she assumed was Lord Orford ask the footman. And yet... Why did she know that voice?

"You have a guest, my lord. A—"

"Well, can you not see that I'm busy with my steward? Send them away," his lordship snapped.

Anwen was affronted, even though she shouldn't care less if Lord Orford wanted to admit her or not. However, he should not speak so harshly to his servants or snap at them just because they were doing what they were employed to do.

"There is a highly polished carriage out front, my lord," another gentleman's voice stated, causing the room to quiet. Footsteps sounded as if one of them were walking to the window. "It appears to be the Viscount Astoridge's coat of arms, my lord."

"What?" More hastened footsteps ensued.

Anwen, without guile, listened at the door, certain she knew that man's voice. Surely it could not be...

"Hell."

The muffled word carried to Anwen, and she gasped when she realized with sickening dread where she knew that voice from.

It could not be.

Without waiting for the footman's return, she pushed open the library door and gaped. As assumed, three men were inside the library, but only one man captured her attention.

A man who ought to be in the stables, mucking out stalls and preparing to meet her later at the lake.

She stepped into the room and fought not to cast up her accounts. "Leave," she commanded, pointing toward the door. The steward and footman gaped at her with shock.

"Miss, I do not think you have the right—"

"Leave, now," she shouted, startling all three of them.

The men turned to Daniel, who nodded, permitting them to follow the order.

Anwen waited for the door to close, giving her time to compose herself.

Daniel...Lord Orford held out a hand, attempting to halt her tirade, which she doubted would be suspended long, not if the anger boiling within her was any indication. Already she could feel her ears growing hot with aggravation.

"Anwen, let me explain."

She snorted, not the most ladylike sound she had ever made in her life, but nor was finding out the man she wanted to marry was a liar. "Oh yes, I'm looking forward to you explaining why you've been pretending to be someone you are clearly not," she seethed, gesturing to him in his superfine coat and highly starched cravat.

He looked the epitome of elegance and gentlemanly handsomeness. She had never had such a bodily reaction to any man before in her life, not before meeting Daniel, so seeing him dressed in tan breeches accentuating his perfect muscular form, broad shoulders, and handsome face was unjust.

"I did not set out to deceive you. I promise you that. I merely ran into you one day, and you just assumed I was someone I was not."

"Oh, so it is my fault that you're a liar. I see, Lord Orford," she spat. "Care to explain why you continued your ruse then? I'm all ears and would love to know."

He walked toward her, and she backed away. "Do not come too close, my lord. I do not think it is safe for you to do so now."

He halted halfway across the library and sighed, running a hand through his hair.

A pang of longing tore through her. She adored his hair, soft and long enough to run her fingers through, which she had done so many times when they were kissing.

Oh, the rogue would not get away with this betrayal.

SEVENTEEN

Daniel's mind whirled with thoughts on how to make the situation right. How to correct his wrong that now threatened his and Anwen's affinity?

Looking back at his farce, he'd been a fool to think she would see his lying as a lark, nothing too bedeviled that one could not forgive.

Anwen stood before him, all enraged beauty, and never had she looked more ravishing and untouchable than she did at this moment.

"You were so different from how I knew you would be should you know who I was that I chose to keep the details of my new title to myself. For a little while at least, although I did not mean for it to go on as long as it has."

She shook her head, the scowl between her brows deepening. Not a promising sign if he were going to win her forgiveness. Damn it all to hell. He hoped he had not done unforgivable damage.

"You allowed me to give myself to you, a man who I thought was a groom! How do you think that makes me feel? I do not know who it was that I loved that night," she said, pacing before him.

The word love reverberated around in his head for a moment before what she said brought him to his senses. "I'm the same man, Anwen. Before inheriting the title, I spent my days idle and without much direction. This world you've lived in your entire life was not a place I thought I'd ever have to navigate. I felt certain the late Lord Orford would marry and sire an heir, and any chance of me inheriting would be a moot point."

"And, what are you trying to say?" she said, stopping her pacing to glare at him. "So inheriting this estate and becoming a marquess has made you into a liar? And do not say you've not known how to live in my world, as you call it. Where were you living before moving to Surrey?"

Daniel cleared his throat, not wanting to delve into his life before becoming a marquess. It did no one any good to remember those nights of debauchery and wickedness. "London, but not your London, I would add."

"You lie, and there is little you can say now that I would ever believe. You have proven to be a man who plays games with others and thinks it's amusing." She paused, crossing her arms over her chest. "Tell me, was our time together a means by which you could force me to marry you? A woman intimate with a servant would provide enough fodder for you to get your way."

Daniel did not reply, merely watched with severe hopelessness as Anwen clasped her forehead and strode to the window, looking out over the front drive. Her silence echoed through the room like a death knell.

"I would never force you to do anything you did not wish to. I would've thought the friendship we cultivated would have at least settled that fear." Daniel approached her, wanting to pull her into his arms, but he resisted. She was angry, shocked, and upset, he needed to give her space, time to accept what had been disclosed to her today.

"I came here today because my brother wished me to welcome Lord Orford to Surrey."

"He did?" The surprise in his tone caught her attention.

She turned, pinning him with a hard stare. "Is that so hard to believe? My brother is a gentleman, after all. My coming here and extending a hand of friendship is the right thing to do, but I suppose you wouldn't know anything about the right thing since you're a trickster who preys on unsuspecting women."

"Your friendship with me before you knew who I was is admirable, Anwen. Not many ladies, even of good character and a kind heart, would give a lowly groom the time of day, but you did."

"I gave you a lot more than that." He watched, his heart beating to a stop, when her eyes filled with tears.

Without thought, he reached for her, wanting to comfort her, but she pushed his hand away, moving out of his reach.

"Shame on me for trusting you, I suppose." Her words cut him deep, and he followed her as she turned and strode toward the door.

"Please do not leave, Anwen. Let us talk this through. I'm sorry I made the mistake of not telling you the truth. I did not mean to hurt you. I know you do not wish to hear it, but I enjoyed our time together. I was able to get to know the real Lady Anwen Astoridge, not the prim-and-proper debutante you undoubtedly are when in London."

"Tell me, my lord, when did you intend to reveal who you really were?" she asked, her tone chill enough to make the room cold.

"I was going to tell you today at the lake."

She threw back her head and laughed. "Were you now." The words rang with sarcasm. "And there, you see, even if you were going to tell me the truth, I would not believe you now. It is too convenient, do you not think?"

"Anwen, please, what I say is true. I do not want this to end what we have together. You're a lady, and I'm a marquess, there is no impediment for us not to continue the courtship."

"Other than the fact you lied to me. Created a fictional world in which you lived and made me believe you were someone else. You are just like all the other gentlemen in town. Popinjays and dandies who care for no one other than themselves and their own self-indulgent wants and needs. You do not want me or what we have to continue. Had you done so, you would have corrected me on the first day we met about who I assumed you to be. Not made me look the fool."

"We've been intimate, Anwen. You cannot just walk away from me, no matter your wish." The moment the words left his mouth, he wished he could rip them back. They were all but a threat. Her face drained of color, and he stepped toward her, wanting to reassure her and correct what he said. "I did not mean..."

"Yes, you did. You mean exactly what you say. That you're now intimidating me should I take a step back from whatever this was between us is deplorable. But you may do your worst, Lord Orford. I will not be bullied just because I gave myself to a man I cared for. It is you who ought to be ashamed, not me."

She turned on her heel, wrenching the door open and storming through it without a backward glance.

He let her go, knowing there was no use in trying to talk

her around, not now, at least. She needed time to come to terms with what she had learned today. Tomorrow he would call on her when she was less hysterical. She may be angry now, but that would pass, and she would soon see that he was the same man, the groom, and now lord that she cared for just as he cared for her.

By the time she arrived home, the anger that simmered in Anwen's veins had become molten, and she could not calm her racing heart for the annoyance and hurt coursing through her.

"Ready the carriage. I'm traveling to London today. We shall go as far as the Bells Inn this evening and complete the journey to town tomorrow."

The butler, his eyes wide, nodded and agreed to her demand.

And good it did him, too, for she would not have anyone talk back to her this afternoon, not after what had happened today.

The lying cur. How could he allow her to lay with him when she believed him to be someone he was not? How he must have laughed at her gullible nature.

All the conversations, her hope of a future together. What had Lord Orford been thinking, pretending to be a groom? She did not buy his excuse that husband-hunting debutantes were why he kept up his farce when she had made the error of his position at the Orford Estate. Who did such a thing and thought it was appropriate?

The Lord Orford did. That was whom.

She made it to her room and stripped her bonnet and gloves. "Pack everything, Mary. We're going to London. The carriage is being prepared now. I will not be staying in Surrey after all."

"Lady Anwen, is everything well? You look pale."

She waved her maid's concerns away. She did not want people to look and feel sorry for her. Thank heavens no one knew of her shame. Not that she was ashamed for giving her heart and soul to Daniel. She grew to care for him, had thought him her friend, a man she had been willing to elope and have a future with.

But to learn all of their companionship was a lie, possibly even a game for Lord Orford, was too much to stomach.

They were the same now, and she would never forgive him for his deception. "All is well, Mary. But my brother requests me to join the family," she lied, not wanting anyone to know why she needed to flee Nettingvale. "My time here has come to an end. Time to travel to London and do right by my family and marry." Marry a suitable, kind man who did not lie or make up ridiculous falsehoods about himself.

"Very good, Lady Anwen. I shall have you packed in an hour, no more. Do you wish to change before you leave?"

"No, this morning's dress will suffice." She walked to the window and looked out over the grounds, refusing to glance down at the terrace where Daniel had kissed her to within an inch of her existence.

Or the lying Lord Orford, whom she would forever think of him from this day forward. He was not fit to hold the title of marquess, blast him.

CHAPTER
EIGHTEEN

London

Daniel lasted a week after Anwen's departure before he had his staff close up the house in Surrey and travel to London—the overwhelming emotion of needing to see her surpassed his need to remain safe in the country.

The town house on Hanover Square was in much better condition than his country estate, and he was thankful much of the staff remained employed when he'd taken over the title of marquess.

He sat in his carriage, staring at the foggy Mayfair streets, and debated how to regain Anwen's trust and affection. She was angry with him, and possibly would be for some time to come, but he was certain that he could make her see he did not mean to injure her feelings, that his affections for her were genuine and heartfelt.

He flipped the small parchment note over in his hands and debated opening the missive. The handwriting was familiar, but one he had hoped to put behind him.

Miss Molly Darling had other ideas. How his past mistress even learned of his arrival in London, he did not know. He'd not been back in town but a day, and already she was writing to him?

He broke the seal and opened the letter, reading the words that jumped out at him like a lure. An invitation to her new villa at St. John's Wood. An interesting invitation, since rumor had it she was under the care of a new protector. There was no reason she ought to be writing to him to warm her bed.

He would not go, of course, but his mind debated the vices he could have in the privacy of her home. The opium, the wine, the pleasure of losing himself in that blissful nothingness, drew a part of him he had fought so hard to escape.

He tore the letter up, throwing it onto the squabs. He would not be lured into a lifestyle that had almost killed him. Nor would he throw away what he could have with Anwen for a past that was no good for him. Should his defenses crumble and he tumble into his rakish past, his future with Anwen would be over before it had a chance to really begin.

The carriage rolled to a stop, and his footman opened the door, lowering the steps. Daniel stepped down, adjusting his superfine coat, one of many he'd had made with haste upon his decision to attend the Season. As he walked into the Georgian mansion, he could feel the eyes of the *ton* upon him.

Some had questions in their inspection of him. Who he was and what family did he hail from, rank, and the value he held in society. He walked through them with his head held high, the promenade reminding him of his first day at

Eton. The boys took his measure, seeing if he could enter their world and be one of them.

He was not allowed to be part of the club then, but he would be now, so fickle were the *ton* and their ways. Soon enough, they would find out who he was and learn of his inheritance that came with the name Orford.

He addressed Lord and Lady Dantes and entered the ballroom, taking in the rectangular-shaped space painted with dark green walls and accentuated with gold leaf mirrors. The candlelight made finding anyone at a distance difficult, yet he tried to make out as many brown-haired debutantes as possible, but could not see Anwen.

There was a chance she had yet to arrive. The lineup after his carriage had been many. How she would react to his presence, he could not guess. Would she force her brother to cut him in society? Would she ignore his attempts at reconciliation?

Although Lord Astoridge had held out the hand of welcome in Surrey through his sister, that did not mean it would continue here in London. Not when he learned what had transpired between himself and his sister. Which he was sure to do if Anwen did not disguise her hostility toward him.

Daniel moved through the throng of guests, greeting the few he recognized before stopping to speak with a group of men discussing this year's top picks of debuting ladies.

He did not contribute to the conversation, merely listened with a disinterested ear before Blackhaven clapped him on the shoulder, a friend from his rakish past that was now happily married.

"Orford, it is good to see you in town. I wondered if you

would attend after only recently inheriting the title. How is everything in Surrey? The late marquess did not come to town, and little news came from the estate during his later years."

They stepped away to speak alone. "It is not the best, I'm afraid to say, although I'm certain it is not entirely lost, and I shall soon have it to rights."

"A wife would help with solving your issue. They do have a marvelous way of running houses and getting them to shine," Blackhaven said, the duke's gaze moving across the room to where his duchess stood speaking to several ladies.

He chuckled and did not mention the only woman he had thought to occupy his life and bed was so enraged with him that she had fled to London to avoid his presence. "I shall keep that in mind."

Daniel sipped his brandy, keeping his attention on the ballroom doors, not wanting to miss Anwen's arrival. Surely she would be here soon. The thought of glimpsing her again, speaking to her, sent a thrum of impatience through him.

Their parting had not been what he had wanted. He did not want them to be distant or for her to remain angry. Too much had passed between them now for them to part ways, not without trying to salvage what they once had.

Not that Anwen thought they had anything after learning the truth, but he would prove to her they did.

A woman bumped into his arm as she passed and almost sent his brandy flying. "My apologies," she murmured, not halting her steps.

"Of course," he replied, glancing in the lady's direction.

His heart stopped the moment he realized who had run

into him. Like a punch to his abdomen, the sight of Anwen almost brought him to his knees.

Tonight she wore a ruby silk ballgown that accentuated her woman's body, lush and ripe for the picking. Under the candlelight, she shone like the jewel she was. Her hair, coiled into curls, sat low on her nape, glittering with the help of the small diamond pins throughout. She stopped and spoke to a woman he did not know mere feet from him, unaware of his presence.

He could not look away. Never had he been speechless, but this night he indeed was.

She was the epitome of perfection, breeding, and beauty, and damn it all to hell, he wanted her back.

Summoning his courage, he sought her to speak, but hesitated when a man joined her small set. His superfine coat and loftiness of speech spoke of breeding and privilege. Daniel's eyes narrowed, not liking the hungry regard in the man's eyes whenever he looked at Anwen—the type of man she ought to marry.

Anwen laughed at something the lord whispered in her ear, and Daniel had never wanted to pummel someone more in his life.

The word *mine* thundered in his mind, and he fought to control his calm visage. The man picked up Anwen's hand and kissed the back of her silk-gloved fingers, and Daniel fisted his hands at his sides.

How dare he touch a single hair on her head, nevertheless kiss any part of her body. The bigger question, however, was why she was allowing anyone to be so familiar with her.

Did she feel nothing for him? Was their time in Surrey meaningless? Surely that was not the case. No one could be so fickle, even if one were incensed.

Anwen placed her hand on the gentleman's sleeve, his lordship escorting her for a dance, and his annoyance doubled. She coquettishly glanced at the man as he pulled her into his arms, and Daniel's patience all but snapped.

He did not move his attention from her, not even when he could feel interested eyes had noted his magnet-like draw, including Blackhaven's. Anwen was swept into a waltz, her smiling, giggling self unlike the woman he had met in Surrey.

Where was the opinionated country lass who had captured his heart? Who loathed this society and the flops that threw unwanted compliments toward her as a means to win her heart.

What had happened to the woman who had not wanted to be in London to find a husband? She indeed appeared as if finding a husband to marry and bed was of the highest priority.

Anwen laughed, the sound carrying to him, and even from the side of the ballroom, he could hear the falseness of her tone. For all her simpering and shy smiles, she was not interested in the man who danced with her.

It was all a lie, much like how she believed his behavior to have been these past weeks.

Her attention moved to those watching the couples dance before her eyes settled on him. He saw the moment she recognized him. Perhaps even in his imagination, he heard her sharp intake of breath.

He ground his teeth, unable to smile, to appear happy to see her, all of which he was. But seeing the bastard lord holding her was too much. He took a calming breath when her dance partner's hand slid lower on her back. Far too low to be appropriate.

The shock slipped from her face, replaced with annoyance.

Daniel shook his head, turned on his heel, and left—better that than what else he had envisioned for the night, which was nothing good.

NINETEEN

He had no right, of course, to be annoyed and feel the jealousy coursing through his blood, but he did. He had made a mistake. Surely Anwen could forgive his error. It was not so bad...

The throng of guests around him became a blur as he made his way out of the room before Anwen, by some trickery, appeared to cross his path yet again.

"Anwen?" he called, clasping her arm and pulling her to a stop.

The woman stared him up and down as if she did not know who he was, and for a moment, he wondered if he had morphed into some alternate universe where they were once again strangers.

Anwen turned to face him, and interest replaced the confusion in her gaze. Hope sparked through him that maybe she was willing to at least speak to him.

"Anwen, am I?" she said, a small smile playing on her lips. A mouth that he had dreamed about kissing again.

"Will you come with me?" he asked. "We need to speak

alone." He held out his arm, and she wrapped hers about him, giving him leave to escort her.

"Let us watch the dancers, shall we?"

He conceded, but in truth, he wanted to take her away from this room, plead his case, and have her forgive him. "Of course, but will you promise to listen to what I have to say? Not run away like you did before?"

"I will listen and hold judgment since we're about society, but I must admit to being intrigued as to what you want to explain."

Daniel halted their progress and stared at her, perplexed. "You know what I have to say. I'm sorry again for lying to deceive you, but I did not do so to hurt you. I enjoyed our time together..." He took a calming breath, remembering their night of passion, of sinking into her sweet heat and scorching both their souls. "I want you in my bed again. I want you as my wife."

Anwen's mouth gaped, and she closed it with a snap, pulling out of his hold. "Lord..."

"Orford." He frowned. "Anwen, you know who I am."

"Well," she said. "I know who you are now, and I also know that my sister Anwen has a lot of explaining to do."

It was Daniel's turn to gape. "Blast, you're Lady Kate?" he queried.

She crossed her arms over her chest, everything weirdly and eerily the same as Anwen. "I am, and now, you were about to explain why my sister knows you so intimately and well. Shall we begin? I'm waiting, Lord Orford."

With all the strength she could draw, Anwen forced a smile and continued the dull conversation with

Lord Freemont. She ignored that Daniel was in London, had seen her, and promptly fled.

His lordship continued his discussion of native trees to England, and his dislike of oaks, in particular, was not a topic close to her heart. Did the man indeed not have anything else to discuss?

What of parliament, the royal family, or the living conditions of the poor that were so often overlooked? But then, she knew why Lord Freemont and so many of his ilk spoke of such boring subjects, because they were under the impression that women did not have brains or independent thoughts that could contribute to meaningful conversation.

You had a noteworthy conversation with Daniel...

Anwen inwardly sighed and kept her attention on Lord Freemont, anyone but the bane of her existence who had fled.

A little satisfaction thrummed through her that her dancing with Lord Freemont put him out. Surely there would not be any other reason why he had stood at the side of the ballroom glowering like he wanted to murder some-one. Namely his lordship. Not that Lord Freemont seemed to notice.

Devil, take the marquess. Orford did not deserve one ounce of her interest after his atrocious falsehood in Surrey. He lost such rights when he lied to her.

She ground her teeth, forcing her smile broader, her eyes brighter with mirth as she danced. How dare he pretend to be a servant. A groom, a man she had opened her heart and soul to. She had given Daniel her trust while all the time he'd been lying to her face.

Lord Orford, indeed. Lord "better keep away from her lest she gives him the cut direct."

The waltz ended, and Lord Freemont escorted her off

the dance floor. Her steps faltered when she viewed Orford had not left. Had, in fact, been stopped on his way toward the foyer by Kate, who was speaking to him.

Lord Freemont suggested a ratafia and set off to supply them both with a repast, but Anwen did not wait for him to return. Her sister's shocked visage told her their conversation was a surprise, and she dreaded what they were saying.

She started toward them, needing to halt the conversation before too much was said. She had not told Kate anything of what had transpired in Surrey. She had been determined to put Daniel and their history behind her.

Shame washed through her that she had given herself to him. She had put herself at risk of becoming pregnant. What had she been thinking to be so reckless with her future?

Should Kate discover her shame, her sister would think her mad for wanting a future with a groom. To be his wife and live a simpler life than the one she was supposed to, and her family could be correct.

But it had been a life she craved, had wanted with all her heart, no matter how difficult the road ahead for them may have been. She was confident in her brother's love that he would not have disowned her. He would not have allowed her to starve or be without a family or home.

Not that she should give another minute of thought to such a future, for it was not to be. Daniel was Lord Orford, a marquess whose future was quite the opposite of the groom Daniel Clarence.

"Lord Orford, you have met my sister, Lady Kate, I see. Kate, this is Lord Orford, our new neighbor in Surrey," Anwen said as a means of interrupting their conversation.

She could feel Orford's gaze on her, her skin aching with

the need to have him touch her, kiss and be with her again. There was something about the man, no matter how angry she was with him, that drew her in.

"Sister," Kate said with a raised, knowing brow. "Lord Orford was just explaining how you both came to know each other. You did not tell me you spent much of your time occupied together in Surrey."

Anwen met Daniel's gaze and glared. "I hope he had not been making more of our time together than he should. We merely encountered each other out riding several times, Kate. There is nothing significant about it."

"Really?" Kate said, her visage becoming hard. "That is not what I heard, especially when poor Lord Orford thought I was, in fact, you when we first met this evening. How interesting that conversation was, my dear sister."

Oh, dear God...

"What did you tell her?" Anwen demanded. "How dare you break my trust yet again?" she asked, knowing far more had been said this evening than she wanted.

"I apologize, Lady Anwen. I did not know you and your sister were identical in appearance."

His formality threw her a moment before she rallied her thoughts. "I told you I have a twin sister. That should be explanation enough not to run your mouth to everyone you meet for the first time."

"Anwen, that is unkind," Kate said, her tone hard.

"I do not care if it is unkind, Kate. I do not wish to have this conversation at all, and certainly not at a ball surrounded by wagging tongues. I was acquainted with Lord Orford and no longer wish to be so. There is no point in you being here, my lord. You will not change my mind about anything," she said, not wanting to go into specifics, especially with her sister listening.

"May I call on you tomorrow then, Lady Kate?" he asked. "Would that be suitable for you?"

"That would be best, my lord," Kate answered before she could get a word in.

"I do not think that is necessary. We have said all that we need to back in Surrey. Or, to better explain, Lord Orford has explained very little, and that is why we are no longer friends."

"We were more than friends, Anwen."

Anwen took a calming breath, ignoring his gravelly tone and her sister's pointed stare. "You may call," she conceded. "But it will change little. Do not expect me to be swayed to change my mind. I do not care for liars or people who use others for amusement."

"I did not do that," Daniel said, reaching for her hand.

She slapped him away. "I'm leaving. Kate, you may come with me or stay. I do not care. But I will no longer stand here and listen to a liar spout more untruths that only serve his selfish means." Anwen started for the foyer, not caring who followed, only knowing she had to leave the stifling room that sucked all the air from her lungs.

Better that than scratch the eyes out of a man who had broken her heart.

CHAPTER
TWENTY

Daniel arrived promptly at the agreed-upon time the following afternoon with a pleasant smile that only irked Anwen more than he had last evening.

His lordship gave his hat and coat to a waiting footman and took a fortifying breath before entering the room. Was he nervous about her treatment of him this day? Did he worry she would send him away and never speak to him again?

As it was, the thought her sister allowed him to call was almost as vexing as his being here, but she would listen to more of his lies, and then she would tell him to leave and never come back. She had been played before by men of Lord Orford's ilk, Mr. Kane coming to mind, and she would not play the fool yet again.

"Lady Anwen. Lady Kate." He bowed, his attention moving to her sister, but a moment before, he'd waited for her to admit his visit.

Anwen flicked through her *La Belle Assemblée*, taking her

time in acknowledging him. Her sister cleared her throat, a sign she had noted her sister's snub.

"Come, Lord Orford," Kate called from where she sat near a window to allow them privacy. "Please sit down."

He did as Kate bade and sat beside her on the settee. The moment he did so, Anwen regretted not sitting in a singular chair that could not be shared.

She allowed the silence to stretch for as long as she could before even she knew something had to be said, if only to end this torturous visit. "You should not have come, Lord Orford. I do not want to see you," she said, wanting to be honest. It was not in her nature to give second chances, and nor did she like being made the fool. How he must have laughed at her gullible nature in believing he was ever a groom.

"You must let me try to repair the damage I caused in Surrey. Truly," he said, clasping his chest. "I only wanted you to be comfortable and natural around me, or I would have told you immediately who I was. But you seemed to enjoy Mr. Clarence's company as I enjoyed yours, and I did not wish for it to end."

"I do not think you know this, my lord, but I have been the plot of men's games in the past. One gentleman pretended to court me while all the time his interest in me was to gain access to my shy friend, to whom he is now married. Everyone thought I would marry the man who turned about and eloped with someone else entirely, so forgive me if I do not trust you or take issue with lies. They detest me. I detest myself after I allowed what happened between us in Surrey to occur," she whispered. "Just leave. I do not wish for you to court me or call again. Once my trust is broken, you shall never gain it back."

Orford frowned, running a hand over his jaw. She

studied his face, pushing down the longing that rose within her seeing him again. This afternoon he was the epitome of the upper class. The superfine coat fit him like a glove, his breeches made of the finest cotton, his Hessians polished so that one could see one's reflection. The urge to run her hand through his hair, pull him close, and kiss him thrummed through her, and she debated her anger.

Maybe he was sorry? Maybe his falsehood was an error.

Maybe you are wrong, Anwen...

"You cannot mean that." He clasped her hand, and something stopped her from pulling away. "We were intimate, Anwen. That alone means as a gentleman, I cannot walk away from you, nor do I wish to."

"So you want to court me, marry me, only because I gave myself to you?" She stood, wrenching her hand free. "I'm not a charity case that you need to save, Lord Orford, and even if I were, you mentioning our escapades in such a way makes me deplore you even more. How dare you?"

"Anwen!" her brother roared from the doorway, striding into the room as if marching toward a battlefield. "You gave yourself to Orford? In what way *exactly* did you give yourself?"

"Lord Astoridge, good afternoon," Daniel said, stepping back from the viscount who appeared ready to murder someone, namely him.

"Do. Not. Speak, Orford, until I hear what my sister has to say to explain her words that I just overheard from the doorway."

"How long were you standing there?" Anwen had the gumption to ask, not cowling to her brother, no matter how enraged he was.

"Long enough to know you should already be married if I heard correctly." Astoridge rounded on Orford. His eyes ablaze with anger. "You will marry Anwen, and soon. Should anyone hear of your conduct in Surrey or, God forbid, you're *enceinte*, you'll be ruined, and your sister along with you."

Anwen gaped and moved to where Lady Kate stood after joining them. They linked hands in a show of solidarity or support, Daniel did not know, but nor did he like to see either of them chastised as if they were children. They were far from that.

"Lord Astoridge, your sister is not a debutante but a grown woman, and I'm seven and twenty, and while we overstepped propriety in Surrey, nothing has transpired here in London that would cause scandal or mean we should marry in haste."

"But *I* say that it has been some weeks since Anwen has returned from the country, and we do not need the mamas of the *ton* calculating the time you were married and the time a child was born, should my sister be pregnant." A muscle worked in Astoridge's jaw, and Daniel considered taking another step from the volatile man. "You will marry, and that is the end of the conversation. I shall have everything arranged forthwith."

Anwen stepped forward. "What if I do not wish to marry Lord Orford, brother? Will you force me into a union I do not care for? I do not love him, and for some time, I have done nothing but loathe the marquess. You cannot possibly punish me by making me marry a man I abhor."

"Anwen," Daniel pleaded, hating that she could say such things about him after all they had shared. He rubbed a hand over his chest, disliking the pain her words brought forth.

"What, Lord Orford, it is true, is it not? You used me, maybe even to ruin me so we would have to marry. Your visit here this afternoon may have been a ruse for you to have my brother overhear our conversation to force such a union between us. I shall never forgive you should you make me marry you."

"You have no choice," her brother thundered. "Neither of you have a choice. You will marry. That is what happens when you're free with your person."

Anwen scoffed, glaring at her brother. "And you were not free with your person. Tell me, brother, were you so chaste with Paris before your marriage? I do not think you were, so do not chastise me on your lofty principles, for I will not have it, you hypocrite."

"Anwen, that is enough!" her brother said, his tone deadly.

Anwen fled the room, Lady Kate following close on her heels, leaving him and Astoridge alone.

"This is not how I wished for our union to commence," Daniel stated, hating that he had caused so much strife in the family. That had never been his intention. Why had he not just been honest?

And there is still more to tell her...

"No, this is an unfortunate start, Orford, and I may never forgive you for your conduct and forcing my hand against a beloved sister. We shall hold a dinner party tomorrow evening to announce the betrothal to friends and family, but know this. You will rue the day if you injure her heart a second time, mistreat her, or raise your voice to my sibling. Do you understand I shall hunt you down and end your miserable soul?" Astoridge asked, his voice deadly in its seriousness.

"I will win her heart and make her happy. Granted, I

made a mistake in Surrey, and she does not wish to forgive me, but I shall win her trust and love, and all will be well. I promise, my lord."

"See that you do." Astoridge left him standing in the drawing room alone. Daniel sighed and went to collect his coat and hat. He would return tomorrow for the contracts and dinner. If he were so fortunate, mayhap he could get a moment or two alone with Anwen. He did not wish for her to be irate with him. She had a good heart, one he was confident could forgive.

And maybe one day, gift to him as he had already gifted his to her.

CHAPTER
TWENTY-ONE

He smiled as Lord Astoridge approached him, his hand outstretched in welcome. "Orford, I'm glad you could attend. Tell me," he said, leading him toward a footman carrying a tray of wine. "Are you ready to appear the besotted betrothed to my sister this evening? Remember what we spoke about this afternoon, and both you and Anwen agreed to be the epitome of besotted fools in love."

"I have not forgotten and will do my part. It is not hard to play a besotted gentleman toward Anwen. I do care for her a great deal."

Daniel took a glass of wine from the footman and took in the room. Not that it helped him at all. Most present were strangers except Anwen, her sister, and her mother, whom he had been introduced to this afternoon. Not that the dowager seemed pleased to meet him or learn why her daughter would be marrying in three days.

"Allow me to introduce you to my wife, Lady Astoridge."

The viscount's words pulled him from his thoughts, and he turned toward a beautiful young woman with striking strawberry-blonde hair. He bowed, giving her his full attention. "A pleasure to meet you, Lady Astoridge."

"The pleasure is mine, Lord Orford. I apologize for not meeting with you this afternoon, but the Season does keep me busy most days," the viscountess stated.

He nodded, having not expected the viscountess to be so friendly and welcoming, especially when—even with her husband's outward charm—Daniel felt the annoyance and disappointment regarding the union that was about to go ahead.

"I'm happy to meet your acquaintance now, my lady."

The viscountess gestured for Anwen to join them. Daniel watched her say something to Lady Kate, her lips pursed in annoyance. "Perhaps now it is time to announce the good news, my dear," the viscountess stated to the viscount.

"Ladies and gentlemen, I would like to announce before dinner this evening that my sister, Lady Anwen, and Lord Orford have formed an attachment and will be married. Thank you for coming this evening, and let us toast and celebrate the upcoming nuptials, if you will."

The guests smiled and sighed in delight at the news, and when Anwen joined him, they were soon bombarded by congratulations and happy reflections regarding their union.

The dinner gong sounded deep in the recesses of the house, and they soon made their way to the dinner table. Unfortunately, he was not seated beside Anwen, but thankfully she was across from him, where he could drink in her presence.

Lady Astoridge caught his attention once they were seated. "What a marvelous turn of events that you're our new neighbor, Lord Orford. I understand the late marquess preferred solitude, but I hope you're not of the same character. We shall wish to see you and Anwen often."

He thanked the footman as a bowl of scallop soup was placed before him, the scent of the sea wafting up and making his stomach growl. "I would never dream of keeping Lady Anwen from her family. You shall see us often."

"There is an observatory, is there not? In the hunting lodge? I'm most curious to see one. Have you inspected the observatory yet, my lord? I hear it is quite unusual."

"Yes, have you seen it yet, Lord Orford?" Anwen asked, pulling the attention of the dinner table toward her.

He met Anwen's sweet, curious gaze, but he knew the truth behind her facade, and her eyes, which shone with annoyance, gave her away.

"I have indeed seen the observatory. The hunting lodge where it is situated holds fond memories for me. Ones that I shall cherish forever."

Astoridge cleared his throat, throwing him a warning glare before smiling. "Shall we eat?" the viscount suggested.

Lady Astoridge leaned toward Daniel, placing her hand on his arm. "In time, the viscount will forgive you, my lord. I beg you not to think we are not pleased that you're soon to be part of our family. Although the circumstances are not what we hoped or expected, there is no denying that Anwen cares for you."

Daniel took in Anwen, eating her dinner and speaking to the gentleman at her side. His eye twitched, noting it was Lord Freemont who had but days ago been courting her himself. "I hope in time she can forgive me. It will be better when we're in Surrey and away from London."

"So you do not intend to stay?" Lady Astoridge asked.

"No, if Anwen is willing, we shall leave the day of the wedding. I do not like London." Or what London had a habit of making him.

He sipped his wine, hoping to quell the annoyance bubbling inside him as Anwen found great satisfaction with her dinner companions.

"You're in love with her," her ladyship stated. "Have you told her yet?"

He choked on his sip of wine and fought not to spew the contents of his glass all over the table. He turned to find the viscountess watching him intently.

"I beg your pardon?" He was unable to think of what else he could say.

"Or perhaps you ought to admit that I am right. My sister-in-law has not disclosed everything to me that happened in Surrey, but I can read a room as well as anyone and can guess. Especially with the wedding but two days from now."

Never had Daniel been spoken to so forwardly before, and he had to give the viscountess credit for speaking without using cryptic directives.

"Even if I were, as you say, in love and wished to say such words aloud, she is not ready to listen or believe anything I have to say. Not yet, at least, but I hope in time I can right my wrong."

The viscountess shook her head, tsk-tsking him. "Oh, what a tangled web we weave when first we practice to deceive. That part of your acquaintance I do know, but all is not lost. So long as you're willing to fight hard to earn what you want."

Her words caught his attention, and he looked to her for clarification. "What do you mean by that?"

"I love Anwen, but she is so very headstrong and determined when her mind is set. I knew she did not want to come to London for the Season, and she ensured she did not by extending the cold she suffered to ensure she remained home. She will make you work hard to win her heart, and there will be times that you will think the fight is not worth it, that she will never be moved or inclined to forgive you. But persist, it is just her nature."

The viscountess paused, her attention moving to Anwen. "I do not know if she told you of her previous Season and the disappointment she suffered, but she does not trust easily or forgive. Astoridge states it's because she was born under a Taurus moon, but I think it's because she does not wish to be hurt again."

Which is what he did. Played a game, and now he must live with the consequences of his folly. "I shall not give up. I'm as determined as she is and will not lose this battle."

"I'm glad to hear it," the viscountess said, picking up her spoon to eat her soup.

He glanced at Anwen and found her watching him. Longing ripped through him. He wanted to go to her, pull her into his arms, and beg for forgiveness. Prove to her he never meant to play a game with her emotions. Conversation thrummed about them, but he could not look away. Heat coursed through his blood, need rushing alongside that emotion.

He wanted her.

He wanted to kiss those pouty lips that had been drawn into a thin, annoyed line all night. He wanted to pull her out of her anger for him, tempt her toward the life they could have, if only she forgave him for his lie.

Lord Freemont pulled her attention away, and Daniel cursed his presence. He needed time alone with her where they could speak. Maybe after dinner, an opportunity would present itself.

That could be the start of a new beginning for them both.

CHAPTER
TWENTY-TWO

Anwen avoided Daniel for the dinner party and most of the after-dinner drinks and impromptu dancing that her sister-in-law thought was a good idea in the ballroom.

Even when she reminded Paris that there would be a wedding breakfast that would include dancing in two days' time, there was no halting her sister-in-law's excitement for the night.

Anwen noted Daniel's location in the room. He stood beside her brother, both of them in deep conversation. No doubt her sibling was yet again bestowing another set down on her betrothed and ensuring he would never lie again.

She felt almost sorry for Orford for a moment until she remembered she had given herself to a man believing him to be someone else entirely.

Who made up such falsehoods and thought they would not injure anyone?

She slipped from the room, making her way toward Paris's small office, where she conducted all the household business while in London. No one ever came into the room except for Paris and the housekeeper, and she would be alone here and not be disturbed. A moment's peace is what she needed.

The door opened before she could sit at the desk, and she stifled a squeal of alarm. "Get out," she demanded. "You're not to be in here, Lord Freemont."

He strode toward her, clasping her hands. "I'm here to beg you to throw Lord Orford over for myself. I've been besotted with you from the first moment I saw you, and I know we can be happy. This marriage to Orford is a farce, and everyone knows his lordship is incapable of true affection. His reputation states such truth."

While Anwen had heard Orford had been wild in London, a rake from all accounts, she had not seen that side of his lordship, not in action at least. Yes, he had lied, but he had never forced or coerced her into anything she did not want to do.

"We are engaged; the notice will be in the paper tomorrow. It cannot be undone, my lord. I'm sorry."

"Please," he said, clasping her face. "Anwen..."

One moment he was holding her. The next, she watched as the earl flew across the room, landing on his bottom beside the small fireplace. "Get out, now, you bastard. How dare you touch one hair on my future wife's head," Orford seethed, his voice low and deadly.

Anwen had never seen him so enraged, and she watched transfixed as his heaving chest and fisted hands calmed when Lord Freemont heeded the warning and fled the room.

"You did not have to be violent with the earl. I had everything perfectly in control." She leaned against the desk, crossing her arms.

Orford slammed the door, snicking the lock before rounding on her. "Is that the type of man you wish to marry? That fop?"

She raised her brow and shrugged. "I may have wished to, but someone took that choice away from me. Not that I'll mention as to whom."

"You think this is comic, Anwen. I do not." He came before her, glaring.

She scowled back, not the least in the mood for him or his jealousy. "Your reaction is amusing. Tell me, Daniel, are you jealous that I formed an attachment to a man knowing who he was and his true name? Unlike someone in this room who cannot boast such things."

He scoffed. "Do be serious, Anwen. I know you have done nothing of the kind with Lord Freemont. Yet, you did form an attachment to me. No matter what you say on the matter."

Anwen felt the muscle above her eye twitch. The man was infuriating and so damn handsome that she loathed the very sight of him. "I feel nothing for you now," she said, wanting to hurt him, to prove a point, although she wasn't sure if that point was for her or Daniel's benefit.

He stepped closer still, their bodies but a breath apart. Her heart skipped a beat, and her stomach clutched with need. She took a calming breath and regretted the action when his cologne overtook her senses.

"I feel nothing at all." She raised her chin, daring him to challenge her further. She could play his game all day and end the victor of their tit-for-tat.

"Nothing?" He clasped her jaw, tipping her face toward his. His gaze took in hers, his eyes settling on her lips. He dampened his. "Why do I not believe you?"

Anwen could not move, nor could she breathe. Why did

he have to touch her? She could keep her distance, remain aloof and unaffected by him, and remain angry if only he did not touch her.

"Why do I believe that should I lower my head just so," he stilled as his lips brushed hers, "and kiss you, that you'll melt like the ices at Gunter's?"

D aniel fought to remain chaste with Anwen. To keep her within arms' reach, but the rogue in him refused to obey. He inwardly groaned when she swayed, and her breasts teased his chest.

Damn, she drove him to distraction. He ached to kiss and revel in her affection, laughter, and sweetness.

"Don't you dare kiss me, Orford."

Was she baiting him? Or would she bite his lip should he close the space between them and do what she told him not to? Without thought, he covered her mouth with his, taking her lips and hauling them both toward distraction.

Her fingers clasped his hair, holding him close, but her grip bordered on pain.

A little hellcat in his arms...

Daniel lifted her onto the desk, stepping between her legs. She did not deny him, her mouth seeking, taking what she wanted. The kiss was hard, punishing, a test of wills where he did not know who would be the victor.

He wrenched up her gown. Her legs were smooth, the silk stockings teasing at what lay just beyond their ribboned ties. She opened for him like a flower under the sun's warmth, and he caressed her cunny. Moisture dampened his fingers, and he had to taste her. He suckled his fingers, meeting her wide, shocked gaze.

"Daniel," she gasped.

He kissed her again. She drove him to distraction, and something told him there was no cure. Not that he wanted one. "Ask me to fuck you. Tell me to fuck you, Anwen," he begged, his cock hard and aching against his breeches.

"Fuck me." The words almost brought him to his knees. He ripped his falls open, clasped her ass, lifted her slightly, and sheathed himself within her cunny.

They moaned, her little mews of enjoyment rocking him to his core. She felt so good, so right, that he did not know how to control the emotions that coursed within his blood.

She lifted her knees, her feet hooking behind his legs, and he could not stop his frantic appetite to make her come. To hear her scream, to feel her pull his own release forward. The thought of such an outcome drove him into her, the table's contents rocking to and fro.

"Daniel," she begged.

The kiss was deep and long. She tasted like wine and wickedness. This was madness, what they were doing and where. Mere steps from where her family entertained, but he could not stop. Would never cease, if only she would allow it.

He pulled out and dragged her off the desk, turning her to give him her back. "Bend over," he commanded, watching with awe as she did as he asked without complaint or argument.

"Lift your skirts." He watched, enthralled, as she tugged them up, exposing the sweet, soft globes of her ass. They were too delicious not to kiss. Daniel bent, bestowing each a small token of his delight of being with her again. His cock, heavy and erect, twitched at the thought of taking her this way.

"I'm going to make you scream my name, Anwen." He

clasped his dick and guided himself into her wet heat. She swallowed him and took him to the hilt. For a moment, he reveled in the feel of her tight quim before thrusting once.

She moaned his name, and he thrust again. Giving her what she wanted, what they both needed. She was too delicious for words, and his mind focused solely on bringing her to release.

He relentlessly seized her. Her body tightened around his cock, and he knew she was close. His balls tightened, and unwilling to spill his seed into her before she reached ecstasy, he guided his hand to where her sweet nubbin ached for touch.

He rolled his fingers against the erect little shell, and that was all it took for her to shatter. Her body convulsed around his manhood, dragging him into release, into incandescent pleasure.

He swore and pumped his seed deep into her willing flesh, wanting to leave a mark on her body so no one would ever think she was anyone's but his. He slumped over her back, their breathing ragged, and for several moments, neither moved.

"This changes nothing," she whispered against the desk.

He closed his eyes and prayed for patience. "Well, I shall just have to change your mind, won't I?" he said. And he would. Maybe not this evening, but she would forgive him before they spoke their vows.

TWENTY-THREE

Anwen sat on her bed, sipping a cup of hot chocolate her maid had delivered before retiring. This evening's dinner had not gone as well as she would have liked. That Daniel had been present and she had to pretend to be excited over their upcoming marriage was not what she had wanted to endure.

He was beastly, and that he had followed her into her sister-in-law's office was not to be borne.

Heat kissed her cheeks at the memory of what they had done in anger. She sipped her chocolate, relishing the milky beverage as the memory of the position Daniel had taken her bounced about her mind.

She had not known fornication could be so wicked and satisfying. It made her determination always to dislike her husband hard to maintain.

"Sister," Kate said, barging into her room and sitting on the end of her bed, the curiosity on her sibling's face something she did not want to answer to.

"Yes, sister," Anwen repeated, unsure what had prompted this late-night tête-à-tête.

"What a wonderful evening for brother and Paris, do you not think? They certainly have many friends, and I thought Lord Orford did a jolly good job of pretending to admire you. Do you not think?" Kate asked, her brows raised in question.

"The dinner went well," she agreed, not particularly liking that her sister believed Orford to be pretending to like her. At this moment, he wanted her far more than she did him.

"But I have to ask," Kate continued. "Where did you and Lord Orford disappear to? When you returned to the ballroom, both your faces were flushed."

Anwen stared into her hot chocolate, not wanting to answer that question. "We had things to discuss, and we argued. There is nothing more to our disappearance than that."

"Really?" Kate scoffed, a grin on her lips. "Well, that is a shame, for I had a little wager with Paris who thought Lord Orford had stolen you away to kiss you senseless, and from your flushed countenance and aversion to telling me what transpired, I think Paris may be right. I suppose, considering I thought you set against him for eternity, that I lost that bet."

Anwen sighed, slumping against the bedhead. "I was determined never to forgive him for lying, but the man makes it awfully hard not to thaw a little more each time we're alone."

Kate reached out and rubbed her foot. "You are so headstrong, Anwen. You have always been so, and determined, but I think you should give Lord Orford a second chance. He followed you to London and clearly wished to win back your affections. Was what he did so very bad?"

Anwen thought about her sister's words and knew deep

down that she would be unable to remain angry with him forever. Not when already she looked forward to the wedding night, to be alone with him, married to him...

"After Mr. Kane, you know I found it hard to trust. I thought Lord Orford, Daniel, was common Mr. Clarence, a groom from the Orford estate. I placed my trust in him, and he lied to me. I suppose I felt like I had been played the fool twice by men of influence and power. A game to be played, with me discarded when it was no longer pleasurable for them."

"I do not think Lord Orford wishes to give up his game if you are indeed whom he plays. He is besotted, Anwen, and you'll be very happily married, even if your beginning was a little erratic. I truly believe this to be so," Kate said.

Anwen nodded, having had whispers of such thoughts herself, especially this evening when Daniel had been so protective, so determined to remind her of what they shared. Desire, affection, jealousy, and everything that she supposed married or courting couples could feel.

"I will try to be less cutting and aloof toward Lord Orford, and when he has groveled enough, I shall forgive him," she said, smiling at her sister, who grinned back.

"I will miss you when you move away, but at least you shall always be close to Nettingvale. Maybe I should also seek a husband who lives in Surrey, and then we shall all be together and close by forever."

Anwen threw her sister a dubious look. "Doesn't Lord Brassel live in Kent?" she reminded Kate, which was a long way from Surrey.

"Well, that does not signify, where Lord Brassel lives, for after asking brother for my hand, he has not asked me. And I must admit, I no longer wish to marry such a flippant gentleman, so finding one in Surrey is still a possibility."

Anwen laughed. "If I could give you one piece of advice, it would be to follow your instincts, and if Brassel will not find the courage and ask for your hand, then that is his loss and your gain. There is a gentleman out there for you. I know there is."

"Well, let us hope he makes an appearance soon. We'll be one and twenty next Season, practically an old maid. No one will want to marry me then."

Anwen shook her head, not believing that for a second. "You will marry, and it'll be grand, you will see."

Kate sighed and stood, walking about her room and inspecting her trinkets on the mantel and dressing table. She picked up her perfume and dabbed some on her neck, the scent of lilies permeating the room.

"Is something else bothering you, Kate?" Anwen asked.

Her sister turned, and Anwen could see she had other things on her mind. "Well, there is something. Are you nervous about being married? The intimacies of marriage seem so foreign to me and disconcerting. Do I have anything to be afraid of?"

Anwen shuffled off her bed and placed down her hot chocolate. She walked over to Kate and clasped her hands. "You have nothing to fear so long as you choose the correct man to be your husband. When I'm not mad at Lord Orford, the few times we've been alone, being with him intimately has exceeded my expectations, if I had any to begin with. He makes me feel so incredible, and you shall feel that too, Kate. I know you will."

"We should go shopping for your trousseau in the morning and purchase the prettiest gown in London for your wedding. If I have to give you up and see you married and living elsewhere, you shall outdo every other bride in town this Season."

137

"I would love nothing more," Anwen said, embracing her sister. "And I shall visit you often, I promise."

"I hope that you do," Kate whispered.

TWENTY-FOUR

He should not be here. Daniel paced the back lawns of Anwen's home, watching his betrothed and her sister discuss whatever ladies discussed before the curtains closed and the windows darkened.

He debated throwing a pebble to wake her, but the trellis and ivy that grew up the back of the house seemed the more sensible option. He climbed up to the first story with nothing to lose except his health if he fell to the flagstone terrace below. Thankfully, the Georgian mansion had a decorative sill band running along the entire edge of the building, which enabled him to crawl.

Daniel did not want to think how nonsensical he looked creeping into his betrothed's bedroom window, or how he would explain to any sensible-thinking person who found him in such a position.

All he needed and wanted to do was explain his past to Anwen before they married.

Making Anwen's window, he made the mistake of looking down to the flagstone below, and his head swam.

The first story did not look all that high from the ground, but from up here was another matter entirely.

He tapped on the window as quietly as he could, hoping not to alert the household of his conduct. The room remained quiet, and he knocked again, louder this time. He heard shuffling before the curtains flung wide, and the surprised but beautiful face of Anwen stared back through the glass.

She unlocked the window and opened it, clasping his arm and pulling him into her room as if she were scared he would fall. The thought had crossed his mind a time or two, and he was happy to be back on solid flooring.

"What are you doing here?" she whispered, moving to her door and snicking the lock.

He went to her, clasped her hand, and pulled her to the settee that sat before the dwindling embers of her fire. Now was the time to tell her and beg for forgiveness. He knew what he was about to say would not be agreeable to hear. "I needed to see you alone so we may talk."

"Talk?" she asked, a frown between her perfect brows. He forgot how much she took his breath away each time he saw her. He prayed what he had to say would not see her fleeing to the hills.

"Talk about what?" she said.

He cringed, hating that his debaucheries meant this conversation had to occur. "There are things about me you must know before we're married. Problems I've had in my past that I've had to overcome that I want you to know about before any more promises are made."

"We all have a past, Daniel. Are you certain this is something I need to know?" she asked him.

He thought about her question, which made him rethink his being here, but he shook his doubts aside. No more lies would be between them. Only truth would suffice. "No, you need to know. I promised I would be honest with you after my mistake in Surrey, and I intend to keep that promise, if you would listen before judging me."

Concern feathered across her features, but she nodded. "Very well, tell me what you must, and I shall not say a word until you've finished."

"Thank you." Daniel ran a hand over his jaw, the stubble prickling his fingers. He should have cleaned up a little before coming here looking a frightful mess. "Anwen, I was a man without purpose during my youth and my early days in London. I thought I had no hope of inheriting the Orford estate or becoming the next marquess. I was ruthless in my endeavors to keep myself occupied, a tumultuous life which often led me to rutting my way through London."

Anwen flinched at his words, her discomfort almost palpable, but she remained quiet, allowing him to continue.

"I'm not proud of the reputation that I acquired. A rake at best, cockish at worst. But even my allure and fixation with the fairer sex soon waned and was not enough. I wanted to lose myself entirely."

"Lose yourself?" She shook her head. "I do not understand."

He slumped back into the chair, ashamed of his past and all he had done. "I need you to know that I overcame my troubles, but that they were there once and may be mentioned in society after we're married."

It was Anwen's turn to wilt into her chair. She crossed her arms, her steely gaze not moving from him. "What else should I know, Daniel?"

How to admit to his wrongs. He shook his head, trying to find the words. "I started to frequent opium dens," he finally blurted. "I could not get enough of that sweet smoke that removed all my concerns. I drank laudanum like wine until I was numb and without peccadillos."

"Numb from what?" She leaned forward and clasped his hands. "What made you want to disappear so?"

"My parents and their lack of concern for me, I believe. They never tended to anyone but themselves, and I practically brought myself up. In a way, I'm glad they're out of my life, for I did not want them to pretend to be interested in my well-being after I inherited the title, especially when they did not care before. They never loved me. I may hide behind a visage of wickedness and carelessness, but it's all a facade. I'm as insecure as a newly debuting debutante taking her first steps at Almacks. The opium and laudanum removed those fears, erased my nerves."

She listened, quietly digesting his words. Her features did not give way to what she thought, and he hated to imagine. Would she loathe him more after his telling her of his darkest days?

"When we met in Surrey, you did not seem at all plagued by these iniquities."

"Because I was not. When I discovered I had inherited the Orford estate, I fought to clear my mind and body of the drugs I was inflicting on myself. I arrived in Surrey and found refuge there in the countryside and eventually with you. I did not think a prettier angel could float before me the first moment I saw you, but it did. I would be lying if I did not say that being here in London was not hard.

"I crave to travel to the East End and lose myself once more in those dens of smoky oblivion, but the thought of you stops me. I do not want that kind of life. I want a life with you." Daniel paused, leaving the chair to kneel before her. "I'm in love with you, Anwen, and I hope you love me enough to forgive my sins and know that I'll be honorable and loyal forevermore. I will never go back to that life, for it is no way to live. You are my future, you and I."

A nwen swiped at the tear that ran down her cheek, and she blinked, trying to clear her vision.

He loved her?

The knowledge filled her with solace and sorrow that he had lived such a way for so long. That he thought his parents did not love him. How could they treat him so atrociously? She sank onto the floor with Daniel and embraced him. "While some of your past surprises me, I'm so sorry for what you've had to endure. I need you to know that when we're married, I will support and fight for you every day for the rest of our lives, even if you tumble a time or two. No one is flawless, not even myself." She brushed her lips against his. "Your parents sound as if they should never have had children in the first place. I'm sorry you felt unwanted and unloved. I do not wish for you to feel that ever again."

"There is one more thing that I would ask of you," he said, his attention dipping to her lips. She moistened them, and his gaze darkened with hunger.

"What is that?" she asked.

"I would like to return to Surrey after we're married and not attend the rest of the Season. London holds so many lures, and I'm only new to halting what was slowly killing me. I need to leave, Anwen, and soon. Will you do that for me?"

She nodded, settling on his lap. "Of course, I shall do that for you. That you came here this evening and told me of your troubles, that you were honest with me, that you love me, how could I deny you anything?"

He threw her one of his cheeky grins that made her smile. "Does this mean you'll forgive me for lying to you in Surrey? I truly did not mean to hurt you, Anwen. I loathed who I was before and did not want you to meet that man. I wanted you to meet the real me, even if I did take liberties with my name. The Daniel Clarence who was introduced to you down by the river is the man I fought to become. Whom I should have always been. I do not wish to be anyone else but him with you."

"I wish you had explained all this to me days ago, Daniel. I feel horrible for making you grovel daily because of the lie. I would have understood had you just told me. I understand now, and I'm sorry too that I thought you were playing with me."

"Never," he said, clasping her face. "I would never play with you."

She met his eyes and could read the sincerity in his words. "I'm in love with you, too," she admitted. "And I could never walk away from you no matter what I may have said differently. And come the day after next, we will be husband and wife and return to Surrey after the wedding breakfast."

"Sounds ideal to me," he said, taking her mouth in a searing kiss that also felt like a promise.

CHAPTER
TWENTY-FIVE

T hey were married at St George's Hanover Square before friends and family, as planned. The day dawned to warm sunshine and a cloudless blue sky with no breath of wind—a perfect day for a wedding.

She wore an empire gown of gold silk and the Astoridge coronet her brother lent her as she spoke the words that would tie her to Daniel forever.

The very sight of him made her chest ache and her breath catch. He was handsome; that was never in question, but now that there were no secrets between them, that he had confessed his love for her, he had grown only more marvelous in her estimation.

A wicked part of her was glad they were leaving for Surrey this afternoon. To be away from town meant endless days and nights of doing whatever they wanted and whenever they pleased. Not having to attend balls and parties that did not interest either of them, anyway.

The wedding breakfast took place at her brother's town house, the guests enjoying the warm day on the lawns and terrace. People milled about, glasses clinking in celebration, laughter, and conversation thrummed about them.

"Thank you for this wonderful day, Paris. I did not think pulling off a wedding of such perfection was possible in three days, but you exceeded my expectations."

Paris embraced her. "It is my honor to host your wedding, Anwen. We're so happy for you."

"Is Dominic really happy for me?" she asked, catching sight of her brother who spoke with Lord Freemont near the refreshments table.

"He was disappointed at first, but his meeting with Lord Orford yesterday went well, and they seem on good terms now. There is not anything to worry about. Your brother only had your best interest at heart."

"I know," Anwen said, squeezing Paris's hand. "Where is Lord Orford, for that matter? We're to leave soon."

Paris frowned, looking about the lawn. Anwen did the same but could not locate him.

"Perhaps he is indoors at present and will return shortly."

Anwen excused herself and went about the grounds, speaking to their guests and enjoying the delicacies that Paris had catered for the event. All the while mulling over where Daniel had disappeared to.

When he did not rejoin the breakfast, concern twisted in her stomach. Perhaps the sun was too warm? Was he unwell?

"Lady Orford," one of the housemaids said, startling her. She had never been called Lady Orford before, but supposed she would have to get used to the title.

"Yes," she answered, meeting the maid's chaotic expression.

"A missive for you from Lord Orford. He asked me to deliver it."

Anwen took the missive. "Thank you." Had Daniel sent her a summons? She grinned, breaking the seal and wondering what mischief he was doing now in sending such a note.

Lady Anwen, condolences, or am I supposed to say congratulations? I would venture the former in this case. Proceed to your room, but with care. Games are afoot, and you're not one of the participants.

For what felt like several minutes, she stared at the words, not comprehending what they meant. Suspicion crept up her spine, and she folded the note, not wanting to alarm any of their guests.

Games were afoot that she was not part of?

Whatever could that mean? She stumbled in her haste toward the terrace, and Paris caught her.

"Anwen, what is wrong? You're so pale. Are you going to be ill?"

Anwen wasn't so sure she would not be. "I just received this note. The maid," she said, looking about the grounds for the young woman who had delivered it but had now disappeared. "Said it was from Daniel, but surely it cannot be true. He would not write such words to me."

Paris took the note and quickly read it. She gasped, catching the attention of Kate, who joined them. "What is the matter? You both looked distressed and need I remind you that this is a wedding, and you are supposed to be incandescently happy."

"The time for jokes is not now," Anwen bit out, starting for the house.

Games were afoot?

Where was Daniel?

She pushed down the apprehension that something untoward was happening. After his explanation the other night, nothing could shock her now when it came to him. She knew all there was to know about her husband.

Surely, he had not lied...

Without waiting for Paris or Kate, she ran through the withdrawing room, past guests who preferred the indoors, and up the main staircase.

"Where are you going, Anwen?" Kate asked, coming alongside her on the stairs.

"I need to change and find Daniel. We're to leave for Surrey soon." She tried to keep her voice devoid of trepidation, but her sister's reassuring glance told her she had failed. Her steps slowed when they came to the first-floor landing and spotted two maids, ears to her bedroom door, giggling at whatever was happening inside.

Kate's eyes went wide, and Anwen wasn't fooled by what had gone through her sister's mind over what they were seeing. It was the same as hers.

Games were afoot...

"Move," Kate demanded of the maids. Anwen came up behind her much-quicker sister to the door. The contents of several glasses of champagne and crabcakes threatened to make a second appearance. She swallowed down the fear that curdled her stomach and clasped the doorknob, turning it.

The room was unlocked. Swinging the door wide, she was met with the sight of Daniel and a woman she had never seen before, naked and asleep in the bed.

The contents of her wedding breakfast did make an appearance then, and she ran to the basin and heaved the contents up. She could hear Kate scream profanities that she had never heard before at Daniel and the unknown woman, but neither of them murmured a reply. Daniel merely rolled over and pulled the woman against him, murmuring sweet words into her ear.

Paris approached and clasped her waist as if she were frightened she would tumble to the floor. Anwen was not so confident she would not. "Close the door, Kate. We do not need the *ton* to know what has happened or see what is before us," Paris demanded.

Anwen stared at Daniel's naked form, his arm casually over the woman's naked chest. Her mind jumped from one explanation or excuse to another.

Why declare himself, state his love, and then do this on the day of their wedding?

She strode to the basin and picked up the large water jug before walking over to the bed, where she tipped the contents over them both. Water spilled everywhere, and a small piece of satisfaction ran through her.

They gasped awake, Daniel kneeling on the bed before he turned to see who and what had doused him in water. Anwen stood with the jug in hand and, without thought, hurled it at his head. He hit it away, the jug bouncing on the bedding before tumbling to the floor and breaking.

"What do you have to say for yourself?" she screamed at him.

He closed his eyes, swayed, looked about the room, and stared wide-eyed at the woman at his side. The lady sat up, not the least perturbed by the water. The smug twist of her lips fired Anwen's temper, making her want to scratch her eyes out.

Before he could answer, he shuffled off the bed as if the devil himself was after him. The way Anwen was feeling right at this moment, she wasn't uncertain she would not stop the god of the underworld if he were.

Heedless of his nakedness, Daniel ran a hand through his hair, staring at the woman on his bed as if he'd never seen her before. Anwen shook her head. Did the man think she was an idiot? What a fool she had been to believe that he would change.

Of all days to be so ruthless, did he have to pick their wedding day?

"Anwen, I do not know why Molly is here. Truly, I do not."

Anwen scoffed in unison with the Molly chit.

"Daniel darling, you know why I'm here and what a memorable event it was." Molly met Anwen's gaze, licking her lips in a way that made Anwen's skin crawl. "Your husband always satisfies, Lady Orford." The woman closed her eyes and sighed in a way that only a courtesan would be bold enough to do in front of ladies. "Always worth the ride, but you know that already."

Anwen felt the sting of tears, and she blinked, unwilling to let some harlot get the better of her, even if her husband had. "Daniel, what has happened here?" she asked again, her tone calm despite her heart beating far too fast.

"I do not know. I remember..." He rubbed the back of his neck. "I had a celebratory drink with Astoridge and Lord Freemont, and then," he frowned, "I did not feel well and came upstairs. After that, I do not know what happened."

"You have no memory of fucking me." Molly slid off the

bed, collecting her clothes. "Typical of these nobs. Always forget where their cocks have been when they're before their wives." She held out her hand. "That'll be ten pounds for my trouble, thank ye."

Kate walked toward the woman and did not abate until the Molly chit was pressed up against the door. "Leave now before the anger I'm experiencing toward my new brother-in-law is unleashed on you."

Molly's eyes flared before she slipped out of the room, and her footsteps toward the servant's stairs echoed down the hall.

"Get dressed. We have guests who expect us to cut the cake and have them wish us well on our journey back to Surrey in an hour. You cannot return to our wedding breakfast naked." Anwen turned on her heel and left, Kate following close behind.

The passage spun, and she clasped Kate's arm, fearing she would swoon. Whatever would she do? That she could not imagine but knew it would have to be sorted and fast since they had a wedding breakfast to finish.

CHAPTER
TWENTY-SIX

Daniel fought to keep his balance as the room spun. He'd been here before, the room certainly, and only last evening, but that was not what he meant. He'd felt this way before, unbalanced, seeing the world through a daze, hearing people speak and yet not comprehending what they were conveying.

He slumped onto a nearby chair and tried remembering how he came to be in Anwen's room. When he had met Anwen's eyes and read the disappointment and betrayal burning within them, he knew he did not deserve her.

What had he done?

His silk breeches, shirt, and waistcoat were thrown in his direction, landing at his feet. "Get dressed, Lord Orford. You need to return to the outdoors and finish this farce of a wedding breakfast. We shall discuss what occurred here later," Lady Astoridge stated, her voice stern and cold, unlike her usual sunny disposition.

The severing as he watched Anwen walk away served a pain through him so intense that he almost cried out. His eyes stung, and he blinked to clear his vision.

What have I done?

His worst fears had come true, and he had broken the trust he had fought so hard to earn from Anwen. He would never earn it back a second time.

He dressed as quickly as he could, stumbling through the vertigo that plagued him. That he had laudanum was no doubt, but how had he come to ingest the drug? He had not touched it in several months... And he certainly knew he had not willingly consumed it.

Daniel looked about the room, seeing the two glasses beside the bed, and cringed. His stomach threatened to cast up his accounts.

Pouring himself a glass of water, he drank it and took several deep breaths, hoping he could return to the wedding not as inebriated as he no doubt appeared.

He found his swallowtail jacket and black pumps and headed for the door. He found Anwen and her family waiting in the passageway, each of their faces so unlike how they had been only hours before when he had repeated sacred vows to Anwen from this day forward.

"For everyone's sake, you must appear the loving couple that left the breakfast not an hour ago. Anything less and tongues will wag, and I'll not have that for Anwen. Do you understand, Lord Orford?" Lady Astoridge said, her command brooking no argument.

He nodded, willing to do whatever it took to protect Anwen.

You slept with a woman who was not your wife. There is no protecting her from that, you fool.

They returned to the breakfast to raised glasses and applause. Daniel smiled, pulling Anwen close, not only because he feared she would bolt, but because the warm summer air caused his vision to blur.

Congratulations rained down on them as they both paid their respects and gratitude to their guests, thanking them for their attendance and felicitations.

"How dare you do such a thing to me," Anwen seethed at his side when they had a moment alone. "We shall depart for Surrey today as planned, but know this," she said, meeting his eyes. "I will never forgive you this day, and I shall never be your wife or live under your roof from this day forward."

Daniel watched her sweep off into the crowd, so beautiful and regal, everything anyone would want in a wife, a lover, and a friend. He shook his head, unable to reconcile how he had come to break her trust yet again.

His actions did not make sense. Surely, he was living a nightmare and would soon wake up.

Lord Freemont stopped Anwen, and his nightmare continued. Perhaps there was no hope for him. He was a lost cause, a man without morals. A rake who reverted to his old ways, even on his wedding day, and heedless to anyone who was injured in the interim.

He did not deserve to be loved. His parents did not think him worthy, and now he had ensured Anwen did not either.

A nwen swallowed the lump in her throat and schooled her features to one of incandescent bliss. The constant felicitations were hard to endure after what had happened but moments ago, falling into conversation with Lord Freemont only made her day worse.

The man was a bore and a little too familiar, even now when she was married.

"Congratulations again, Lady Orford. How happy you must be, and soon on your way to Orford House, I understand." He sipped his wine, watching her more intently than she wished, especially when all she wanted to do was crumble into a heap and cry.

"That is right, my lord. We leave London this evening."

"Hmm." He raised his brow, glancing across the lawns to Daniel, who swayed near a blueberry bush. Anwen watched her husband, a pang of longing, of lost hopes making her heart crumble in her chest. How could he have broken her conviction in him after promising never to do so?

It did not make sense. Why would he need to bed his ex-mistress? She was his wife now, a woman who was more than willing to warm his bed. Why run back to a life that he no longer wanted? Why lie to her about what he desired for their future only to throw it away the following day?

She frowned, her mind at sixes and sevens over the matter.

"You appear unsettled, my lady. I hope you're not already having marital woes." Lord Freemont chuckled, and the glee in his tone caught her interest.

"Why would you think so, my lord? Is there something you're aware of that I am not?" she asked in as light-hearted a manner as possible, even though a little part of her wanted to make him squirm.

"Not at all, in fact, should we join Lord Orford to toast your happy occasion?" Lord Freemont started toward Daniel, and Anwen followed. The earl took a glass of wine from a footman and, joining Daniel, handed him the crystal glass.

"Lord and Lady Orford," Lord Freemont said, raising his glass. "May your life be happy and fulfilled." Lord Freemont caught her eye, and she did not like the malicious twinkle within them.

Surely, his lordship did not harbor hopes for them romantically. Although he had been interested in her, he had never declared himself as he should have. And she would certainly not entertain the idea of a tryst, not even after catching Daniel in a compromising position.

Daniel sipped the wine, joining in with the toast. Anwen disliked the facade they needed to portray, albeit necessary, at least until they returned to Surrey.

Daniel cleared his throat, and Anwen looked at him, expecting him to say something to end the awkward silence that had settled between the three of them.

Except, he did not.

He swayed, reached out for support that was not there, and fell to the ground at Anwen's feet. Fear replaced her anger, and she dropped her wine, kneeling beside him.

"Daniel! What has happened?" She rolled him onto his back, her brother coming to kneel on the other side within moments.

"What has occurred, Anwen?" Dominic asked, tapping Daniel's cheek in an attempt to raise him. "Wake up, Orford."

"I do not know. We merely toasted our marriage, and he collapsed." Anwen looked about the grounds, seeing Lord Freemont doing nothing but staring at Daniel with indifference. "Fetch a doctor, my lord," she ordered him. When he did not move, merely continued to be an unuseful cur, her patience snapped. "Now!" she demanded.

The Duke of Holland and Romney joined them, each of the men helping to pick up Daniel. "Carry him into the library. There is a daybed in there," she suggested, leading the way.

Upon entering the house, she caught sight of her lady's

maid. "Mary, have the smelling salts brought in along with water and cloths."

"Yes, my lady," Mary said, running off to do her bidding.

They entered the library, and Anwen sat beside Daniel on the day bed. His face was serene in sleep, yet his coloring was off, gray and drawn. She placed her hand on his chest, needing the security of his heartbeat against her palm, and waited patiently for the doctor.

Her maid bustled into the room soon after with all that she requested, and she dampened the cloth and placed it over Daniel's brow. The smelling salts did little to rouse him, just the slightest flickering of his eyes and nothing more.

"What do you think occurred?" Dominic asked, watching Daniel for any signs of vitality.

"I do not know. He was better," she said, not wanting to get into the details of what had happened within her room.

"Better?" her brother asked. "What does that mean?"

Anwen watched as Paris placed a hand on Dominic's arm, shaking her head as if to halt his questioning. Her brother seemed to understand, but Anwen knew there would be questions later, but right now, all they needed was the doctor.

Wherever the hell that blasted man was.

CHAPTER
TWENTY-SEVEN

The doctor arrived and ordered everyone out of the room while he attended to Daniel with a young man, his apprentice Anwen assumed, following his every lead. With what occurred out on the lawns, most of the guests had departed, bar the few close friends of Paris and Dominic's who remained, along with Lord Freemont, who had fetched the doctor with his carriage.

Lord Freemont leaned against the stairs, a disinterested look on his features that stirred her curiosity. "Thank you for bringing the doctor here, my lord," she stated, disliking how his lordship seemed to enjoy Daniel's collapse, even though she doubted he would ever admit it.

"Anything for you, Lady Orford, but I must say, your husband ought not to indulge so heavily in one sitting. Reminds me of when he was running about town, heedless of his actions or those he injured while enjoying himself."

"You knew Lord Orford before he inherited the title," she said, not a question, merely stating a fact. "I know of my husband's past, my lord. You do not need to hint at his vices as a means to warn me."

His lordship shrugged. "You knew very well that I wished to court you, marry you if you were willing, but alas, I was too unhurried, perhaps acted the gentleman too much for your liking, and missed my chance."

"My liking?" she stated, the pit of her stomach turning at his choice of words. "I do not know what you mean."

"Well, Orford is a rake, through and through. He loves nothing more than games regarding the fairer sex. You were one such game until he found something else to play with."

Lord Freemont's use of the word game bounced about in her mind, and she wondered... Surely, he had nothing to do with what had occurred to Daniel outside or earlier in the day upstairs.

"You do not like Lord Orford, I gather. I wonder why you're here at all, my lord," she said.

"I should probably leave," he said, pushing away from the stairs and bowing before her. "Good luck with Orford, my lady. I fear you shall need it."

Anwen watched him leave, glaring at him as he left before the door to the library opened, and the doctor stood before them. "You may come in now, Lady Orford, Lord Astoridge, too. We must speak."

Apprehension crawled up her spine, and she all but ran into the library, relief pouring through her at the sight of Daniel on the daybed, his chest rising and falling with each breath and, thankfully, a little color on his cheeks.

The doctor closed the door, ensuring privacy. "Lord Orford has ingested a large amount of laudanum, I believe. In a sense, he overdosed and is suffering the consequences." The doctor turned to Anwen, pity in his aging eyes. "Did you know his lordship was partaking in such deceptions, my lady?"

Anwen sat beside Daniel and clasped his hand. "I knew

before he became Orford, he indulged, but not for some time. Not since he inherited the title several months ago. He told me this himself."

"Well, today, he has had more than he should. We have been able to get him to drink some water mixed with charcoal, which will hopefully either make him ill or absorb some of the laudanum, but I suggest you try to persuade him for his health to not indulge again."

"We shall ensure he does not, Doctor," her brother stated, his mouth drawn into an annoyed line.

"I will go to the kitchens if it pleases you and partake in a cup of tea. I do not wish to leave until I know his lordship is well enough for me to do so."

"Of course," Dominic said, guiding the doctors out. The moment the door closed, her brother rounded on her. His face contorted into an angry mask full of rage she'd never seen before.

"How long have you known this of Orford?" he asked, his tone lethally low.

"Daniel told me everything of his past before our marriage. Neither of us wished for secrets to be between us before we wedded."

"Well, he does not seem to care what he says if this is how he acts on your wedding day. We must annul the marriage. I will not have you married to a man who cannot control or stop what does not help him in any way. He does not deserve you, Anwen."

Anwen shook her head, the whole situation, not just Daniel collapsing but what occurred in her room, making little sense. "There is something wrong, I know there is. I can feel it."

"Yes, your husband is addicted to laudanum, and who knows what else."

"No," she argued. "That is not what I mean. I feel like Daniel has been the victim of tomfoolery." Lord Freemont's words, his sly amusement at Daniel collapsing, replayed in her mind. "I think Lord Freemont has something to do with his condition, Dominic."

Her brother also sat on the daybed, thankfully not dismissing her concerns as a woman's fanciful hopes. "I received a note during our wedding breakfast," she continued. "Not long after we arrived from the church." She handed the missive to her brother, who skimmed it.

"What does this mean?" Dominic asked.

With nothing left but to state the truth, Anwen told him of what had occurred upstairs, how she had found Daniel and his ex-mistress. He stared at her as if she were a stranger when she finished telling all that he needed to know.

Anwen reached out for his hand and clasped it tight. "I'm not sure Daniel did anything with the woman in his bed, Dom. And after his collapse outside, I think I'm certain of it."

"How can you be?" he asked.

"Lord Freemont said something to me in the foyer about games Daniel liked to play, and yet the word was also written on the note the servant handed me. Do you not think that odd?"

"It could just be a coincidence."

Anwen shook her head, not believing that for a moment. "No, I do not think so. I think Lord Freemont was behind trying to force an annulment between me and Daniel. We both know he wished to marry me, but had not acted swiftly enough to ask." She paused. "Do you, by chance, have any letters or correspondence from Lord Freemont that we can check the writing against? Maybe we could match it and then know for certain that he is causing trouble out of spite and jealousy."

Her brother sat a moment, his brow furrowed in thought before his eyes widened with hope. "I do, as a matter of chance. We played at Whites several weeks ago, and he lost quite a sum of money and wrote out an IOU to me." Dominic went to the desk and rummaged through his top drawer. "Here it is," he said, waving it in the air.

Anwen joined him, and they laid the note and the IOU side by side on the mahogany desk.

"I will ruin him," Dominic stated.

Anwen nodded, not believing what she was seeing but also so thankful that she was. "They match. Certain lettering is the same."

"Which means that Freemont is in on trying to ruin what you have with Orford by using his past against him and trying to persuade you he has not changed." Her brother paced between the desk and the window. "Do you remember the woman who was in your bed? A name, how she appeared, a birthmark, or anything I may recognize her from?"

Anwen thought over her brother's words, her mouth pursed. "Her name was Molly, that is all I know."

"Miss Molly Darling. She is, and I'm sorry if this upsets you, sister, Orford's ex-mistress from St. John's Wood. But she has a new sponsor now, so she must have been paid a pretty penny to do such underhanded bidding."

Anwen swallowed the bile that rose in her throat at the thought of Daniel being intimate with any other woman, not just Miss Darling. It was one thing to know of lovers in a husband's past, but to come face to face with them and have them gloat before you was quite another.

"I will go and see what she has to say for herself. We

shall get to the bottom of this mess." Her brother started for the door. "Remain here. I shall return soon."

Anwen sat beside Daniel and rinsed the cloth that sat upon his forehead. He did not stir, merely slept, and she hoped Dominic would return with news so that when Daniel woke, she could tell him all that they had learned.

He would not have been so cruel to betray her. He loved her, not his past mistress. She had to be right about Lord Freemont and his meddling ways, and if she was, well, he would certainly feel her wrath the next time she met with him.

How dare he ruin what was supposed to be their happiest day? Not to mention making Daniel ill merely to procure a lie. Well, that was the worst form of duplicity, if ever there was.

And Lord Freemont would rue the day he ever met her should she be right about his deception.

TWENTY-EIGHT

After several hours, Dominic had yet to return from Miss Molly Darling's residence outside of London. Nor had there been any change from Daniel, which even she could see from the doctor's worrying expression was not expected.

From the library window, Anwen observed as the lamp-lighters walked about Mayfair, illuminating the street lamps as dusk soon turned to night. She turned and observed Daniel, praying that he would wake up soon.

She could not lose him now, not on their wedding day, and not when she was sure he was innocent in what had occurred today. Even if his ex-mistress refused to admit to any wrongdoing, Lord Freemont certainly wasn't without blame.

The door to the library swung wide, and Dominic entered, Paris in tow. "She admitted to everything, Anwen. You were right, Lord Freemont was involved. He wanted to make you believe Orford had slipped into his old ways. I suppose in the hopes of marrying you himself by shaming you and ruining a marriage before it even began."

Anwen slumped onto the daybed where Daniel lay. How dare Lord Freemont stoop to such a level. His actions were far from gentlemanly behavior. Not to mention the danger he had placed Daniel in.

She clasped Daniel's hand, wishing he would wake so she could tell him she was sorry, not only for not trusting in him but for being used in such a way.

She knew very well what it was like to be used, and it was a feeling she would not wish anyone to suffer through.

"How dare Lord Freemont treat you both this way, not to mention in our home, Dominic. I will ensure he's ostracized from society and never made to feel welcome again after his atrocious actions," Paris seethed, arms crossed as she looked over Daniel lying unconscious on the daybed.

"I can only hope that Lord Freemont's actions have not caused permanent damage to Daniel. What if he never wakes up, Dom? Whatever will I do?" The tears she had been willing away slipped free, and she wiped them with the back of her hand. "We were angry with each other, or at least I was angry, and Daniel was confused. When he appeared as bewildered as we were finding Miss Darling in bed next to him, I should have known something was off. He promised me he had changed and would do everything to prove that he could be trusted. I should have believed him."

Dominic embraced her, rubbing her back in the way he used to when they were little and had fallen over on the lawns and scraped their knees or hurt their pride.

"He will wake up, Anwen. He's a strong, healthy man who loves you. What man would not fight to come back to you?"

"Anwen..." The hoarse murmur of Daniel's voice pulled her from Dominic, and she clasped his hand.

Relief poured through her at the sight of him awake, his blue eyes focusing on her for the first time in hours. "How do you feel? You have been asleep for hours, and it is now night."

"I shall fetch the doctor from the kitchen," her brother stated, leaving them alone when Paris threw her a comforting smile and left.

"Doctor?" Daniel queried, his brow furrowed.

"You collapsed on the lawns at our wedding breakfast. Do you not remember?" He shook his head, and she continued, "We did not know what was wrong, and so we fetched the doctor. We have since discovered that Lord Freemont had spiked your wine twice." Anwen paused, shame washing through her that she did not believe him that he had changed. But then, what sane woman would not jump to such conclusions with the horrible sight she had been unfortunate to see? "Miss Darling was part of Freemont's plan to make me regret marrying you, not him. He staged you in bed with your ex-mistress." Anwen shook her head, unable to fathom such jealousy. "I suppose he hoped I would annul the marriage and choose him when he came to my broken-heart rescue."

"How did you find all this out?" Daniel asked, attempting to sit up. "I did not take you for a Bow Street Runner," he teased.

Anwen chuckled for the first time in hours, the small glimmer of hope and relief allowed her to feel carefree and without concerns. "It was something Lord Freemont said similar to the note I received that led me to find you in my room this morning. It made me question whether he did not have anything to do with your actions. Finding you alone with Miss Darling was atrocious, but when you collapsed a second time, I knew something was not right. Nothing made sense."

Daniel leaned forward, clasping her face, his palms warm and comforting. "I promised you that I had changed, would not revert to my old ways, and will not. It was laudanum that I've been given, I know the symptoms. Lord Freemont will be lucky if I do not call him out and shoot him dead at dawn."

"No, do not do that. While his lordship deserves a thorough beating, do not allow him the opportunity to take you from me again."

"I do not want anyone but you, Anwen." Daniel brushed his lips against hers. "The sight of Molly turned my stomach, and the look on your beautiful face at the betrayal you thought me capable of made me want to perish. I do not ever want to see you so broken again. I'm not a man who goes back on his word. I promised you love and a life that would be full, happy, and content, and I intend to keep that promise."

Anwen sniffed the tears back. Daniel embraced her, muffling her little sobs, and she reveled at being back in his arms. She lay beside him, never wanting to move from where they were.

"I think," he said, one hand idly making circular motions on her hip. "We should retire after the doctor sees me and enjoy our first night together as husband and wife."

Longing pooled at her core, and she wanted nothing more than to withdraw and be alone with her husband. She was about to suggest they leave when the door opened, and the doctor and Dominic walked in.

Anwen shuffled out of Daniel's arms and allowed the doctor to check her husband. The inspection took several minutes before the doctor turned to her and her brother with a pleased smile. "While I believe his lordship still has some laudanum in his body, there will be no lasting injury to his person. I think it is safe for me to return home, but do send for me again if you're concerned about anything." The doctor turned to Daniel. "You may have a headache come morning, so might I suggest a tisane to help with that, and nothing more."

"Of course, Doctor, and thank you for all you've done today," Daniel stated, climbing off the daybed to stand. He wobbled, and Anwen went to him, not wishing for him to fall.

"A good night's sleep is what I suggest." The doctor threw them both a pointed stare, and Anwen had the overwhelming urge to chuckle.

Dominic walked the doctor out, leaving them alone at last. "Come, we shall go upstairs," she said.

"Let us return to our home on Hanover Square. I do not wish to return to the room that injured your heart today. I want our first night to be where we shall always sleep, where our life will begin, not where someone tried to prevent it."

Anwen rang the bell for a servant, more than happy with Daniel's idea. "I think that sounds heavenly."

The playful wickedness she loved so much returned to his sweet blue eyes. "As do I, my love. As do I."

CHAPTER

TWENTY-NINE

aniel swooped Anwen up in his arms at the threshold of their suite of rooms at his London town house and carried her into the bedroom. He kicked the door closed with his foot, ensuring they were finally alone.

The room was prepared just as he had ordered before the morning wedding. The fire burned bright, and a bottle of chilled champagne sat beside the bed and two crystal glasses to celebrate their marriage.

Not that he had any time for drinking, not at this moment. Right now, all he could think about was having his wife in his bed, his to please and enjoy.

All. Night. Long.

She laughed as he tickled her before slipping her along his body to regain her feet. Her penetrating blue eyes widened, innocent and unaware of how she made him feel. How much he wanted her. His bulging manhood was proof of that.

She threw him a knowing smile that set his blood on fire and sauntered about the room, running a hand over the furniture, taking an interest in the small collection of books he had near his dressing table, and then the bed.

Was she trying to drive him insane while waiting for her to be ready?

She stood beside one of the four bedposts, her eyes taking in the opulent blue bed linen embroidered with the Orford family crest, the abundant pillows he had always thought were an extravagance he did not need.

"So, now that we're here and I'm your wife, whatever will you do with me?" she asked, eliciting all kinds of dirty, enjoyable acts of which he could instruct her.

"I promise to teach you everything, my love." He closed the space between them and covered her mouth with his. Her skin was soft, smelling of florals, and delectable enough to devour. He lifted her against him, carrying her to the bed. She did not shy away from the kiss and threw herself into their shared passion and intimacy.

On the bed, it took all his effort not to toss up her gown and take her in quick succession. She made his blood burn with wildfire, untameable and nothing like he'd ever known.

"You undo me, Anwen."

She whimpered when he kneeled between her legs, tossing up her skirts to pool at her waist. Her sheer drawers teased at what lay beneath. He stripped her of them, revealing what he longed to taste.

He settled between her legs, and her eyes went wide. "You cannot possibly think to...to..."

"Oh, I do think to." His first taste of her made his mouth water. She gasped at the touch of his tongue, mewling his name when he kissed her well. He teased and stroked the engorged button that begged to be petted until she lifted against his mouth, appealing for more.

He would give her more—anything she wanted.

Her fingers spiked into his hair when the first tremors of her orgasm ripped through her. He suckled, wrang out, and enjoyed every moment of her pleasure as it echoed through her. She tasted sweet, and he longed to have her again.

She watched him through her lashes, her eyes heavy with satisfaction.

"Now it is my turn," she said, quickly sitting up. She pushed him onto his back and made short work of his breeches, ripping his falls open and dragging them down his legs.

He kicked off his black pumps, the rogue in him wanting to know what she thought to do. Would she do what he had fantasized most about with her mouth? He shivered.

God, he hoped so.

She was so beautiful, a Siren. His enchantress. His wife, from this day forward.

Her eyes moved over his body, her hand following the same direction of her gaze. She teased his nipples with her middle finger, and she grinned when he chuckled.

"I want to please you too." Her palm brushed over his cock, and he couldn't help but smirk when his manhood bounced before her eyes.

"So smooth and silky." Her fingers ran along his dick before she wrapped her hand around him and stroked.

He groaned, closed his eyes, and savored the sensation. After a quick study, she did it again, sensing his enjoyment. And then he felt it. The flick of her tongue against the head of his manhood before warm lips encircled him and took him deeper into her mouth.

"Fuck, Anwen." He clasped the bedding to stop himself from grabbing her hair and pushing her down, making her take him deeper. But he did not have to; for within a moment, she had taken him deep, his cock hitting the back of her throat as she sucked him with expert precision.

She moaned, and the vibration almost sent him over the edge. She worked his dick with her hand, her mouth. How did she know what to do? How could he be so blessed to have found a wife willing to receive and give pleasure equally?

His balls tightened, his cock strained, and he knew he was close. He lifted her from him, her mouth making a pop as she released his dick.

"You want me to stop?" she asked, a small pout on her reddened lips.

"No, but I want to fuck you first."

She bit her lip, and his cock twitched in need. "I like the sound of that."

A ruthless, wild look entered Daniel's eyes, and he ordered her to turn around. She quickly did as he said, the expectation in her body, the aching, wet need between her legs almost embarrassing.

He clasped her stomach and pulled her against his chest. His cock sat against her bottom, and he pressed against her, rubbing his manhood along the crack of her derriere.

"Lift yourself onto me." She did as he commanded, and his manhood entered her from behind, stretching, filling her with satisfaction.

She moaned and soon learned the way of the position, raising herself before impaling down on his engorged cock.

He was so big and satisfying. His arm wrapped about

her waist, the other nursing her breast, his fingers rolling her nipple.

Sensation shot from her breast to her core. She ached, her body not her own. He pumped into her, controlled her, and pushed her toward another release that she knew would be more shattering than the last.

"I love you so much, Daniel." She held on to him as she took her pleasure. And then she was there, catapulting into heavenly bliss. He hissed out a breath as her cunny convulsed around his manhood.

He bent her forward, on her hands and knees, and pumped ruthlessly into her. She called out as his motions prolonged her orgasm and teased at more to come.

It was too much; she could not catch her breath.

His hands held her hips, his fingers biting into her flesh as he took her ruthlessly.

"I love you," he gasped, pumping into her frantically. He stilled as heat swept into her core, and she knew he had found his pleasure. Daniel groaned her name, and she came again, gasping, pushing, and seeking the last of her pleasure to the very end.

They collapsed onto the bed together. Daniel pulled her into the crook of his arm, and she lay sated and satisfied for several minutes.

When she thought herself capable of coherent speech, only then did she look up and meet his eyes. He watched her, a small, satisfied grin on his lips.

"That was utterly, incandescently amazing, husband. I look forward to learning more of what you can show me."

He chuckled, his hand idly drawing on her back. "I look forward to showing you more. I do not think I'll be able to keep my hands from you."

She grinned, liking him saying so. "You will hear no complaints from me."

They were silent, lost in their thoughts and satisfaction before Daniel broke the hush. "I'm sorry you had to face the challenges of today when it was supposed to be a happy occasion."

She leaned over him, meeting his eyes. "I'm sorry, too, for everything. I was angry with you because you lied, but I should have let it go. But I felt like you were treating me like Mr. Kane all over again, and I suppose I felt the fool."

"You were never my fool. I merely wanted you to know the new me, not the rakehell who prowled London before I met you. I liked being free of expectations and wealth, to be merely common Mr. Clarence, and that you liked me too. What a boon I had not thought to ever gain."

She nodded, understanding perhaps for the first time that in both their ways, their reasons were valid, but came at the expense of the other's feelings.

"I will never break the trust you have in me. Never," he declared, his tone full of determination and truth.

She leaned forward and kissed him. "And I shall never jump to conclusions, and I will always trust in your love and affection."

"Well, I should hope so," he teased, tickling her. She squealed, and he took the opportunity to roll her to her back, coming to lay over her. "And now I feel you need more tutelage in the art of wife."

Anwen wrapped her arms around his neck, pulling him close. "Then you're lucky I'm a willing student. Do commence your education, husband," she teased.

"Oh, I intend to, until death do us part."

EPILOGUE

Four years later, London

A nwen stood beside her sister Kate, Daniel on the opposite side as her sibling laid her husband of only three years to rest. Poor Lord Brassel did not deserve to fall as ill as he did and then pass away at nine and twenty.

She glanced at her sister, her features devoid of emotion, but then she did not expect her to lose her composure so publicly. Her sister had been fond of Lord Brassel, and although the marriage had not been a love match, it did not stop them from being great friends.

Her son, now the Earl of Brassel, stood before his mother, his little two-year-old head bowed. Not that Anwen thought the boy knew what was happening or why, but he sensed the day's misery.

The service ended, and Anwen led Kate toward their carriage, Daniel hoisting little Lord Bassel in his arms and following on their heels.

"All will be well, sister. In time, your heart will heal."

Anwen turned to look at her sweet nephew. "And you have Oliver. He will keep you busy and help you through this hard time."

"The doctor is saying it was some cancerous tumor in George's body that killed him. But it all happened so fast, Anwen. I still cannot process that only last week he was here, and now he's buried, cold in the ground, and we'll never see him again."

They climbed up into the carriage just as her sister gave way to her emotions and cried.

Daniel settled beside her, a solemn look on his face. "I suppose this is not the time to mention that the Duke of Montague called yesterday afternoon, and his meeting with me was most concerning," he whispered to Anwen.

She shook her head, but curiosity got the better of her a minute later, and she had to know what the duke wanted. "Are you friends with the duke? What do you think he wants?" she asked, having never heard His Grace mentioned before.

"No, I only know of him, not know him personally, but he was Lord Brassel's closest friend. He left London soon after Kate married his lordship three years ago. He has not been back, but he is now. Did you not see him at the funeral just now? I should imagine he'll return to Kate's country house for a repast with the other mourners."

"You still have not answered my question," Anwen stated, one curious brow raised. "What does he want with Kate?"

Daniel's lips thinned into a displeased line, and fear shivered down her spine. "He mentioned a debt that Brassel owed but would not elaborate on how much it was. He questioned when Kate would be well enough for callers. I had the impression he now wishes for her to take on the debt and possibly pay up as soon as can be."

Anwen bit her lip, not liking the sound of debt. Certainly, Kate had not mentioned such a financial loan to anyone. Oh, she hoped that the late Lord Brassel had not put his family's security at risk.

"Perhaps it is nothing, and we're worrying over something that does not exist except in our fanciful thoughts."

Daniel scoffed. "I do not know. The way he looked at your sister at the funeral, well, he looked pained and determined all at once. It was quite peculiar."

Anwen thought on her husband's words. Maybe the duke was feeling guilty about whatever he would be speaking to Kate about. Maybe he did not care and was merely inconvenienced by Lord Brassel's death...

"We shall hear soon enough if he does call on Kate. But she's in mourning now, it may be several months before she accepts visitors. I heard her say she's not returning to London but will stay here in Kent."

"Hmm," Daniel murmured. "Something tells me that the duke will not wait months, if he will wait at all, and being here in the country or London, I fear, will not keep that wolf at bay."

The word wolf reverberated in her mind, and she did not like the idea of her sister facing such a prospect. But then Daniel had mentioned the duke being Lord Brassel's friend. Maybe he was here to help, to comfort.

She would take solace in those surmises until she knew differently. Kate was a grown woman. She could take care of herself.

She hoped...

DON'T MISS TAMARA'S OTHER ROMANCE SERIES

The Wayward Yorks

A Wager with a Duke

My Reformed Rogue

Wild, Wild, Duke

The Wayward Woodvilles

A Duke of a Time

On a Wild Duke Chase

Speak of the Duke

Every Duke has a Silver Lining

One Day my Duke Will Come

Surrender to the Duke

My Reckless Earl

Brazen Rogue

The Notorious Lord Sin

Wicked in My Bed

League of Unweddable Gentlemen

Tempt Me, Your Grace

Hellion at Heart

Dare to be Scandalous

To Be Wicked With You

Kiss Me, Duke

The Marquess is Mine

Kiss the Wallflower

A Midsummer Kiss

A Kiss at Mistletoe

A Kiss in Spring

To Fall For a Kiss

A Duke's Wild Kiss

To Kiss a Highland Rose

To Marry a Rogue

Only an Earl Will Do

Only a Duke Will Do

Only a Viscount Will Do

Only a Marquess Will Do

Only a Lady Will Do

Lords of London

To Bedevil a Duke

To Madden a Marquess

To Tempt an Earl

To Vex a Viscount

To Dare a Duchess

To Marry a Marchioness

Royal House of Atharia

To Dream of You

A Royal Proposition

Forever My Princess

A Time Traveler's Highland Love

To Conquer a Scot

To Save a Savage Scot

To Win a Highland Scot

A Stolen Season

A Stolen Season

A Stolen Season: Bath

A Stolen Season: London

Scandalous London

A Gentleman's Promise

A Captain's Order

A Marriage Made in Mayfair

High Seas & High Stakes

His Lady Smuggler

Her Gentleman Pirate

A Wallflower's Christmas Wreath

Daughters Of The Gods

Banished

Guardian

Fallen

Stand Alone Books

Defiant Surrender

A Brazen Agreement

To Sin with Scandal

Outlaws

ABOUT THE AUTHOR

Tamara is an Australian author who grew up in an old mining town in country South Australia, where her love of history was founded. So much so, she made her darling husband travel to the UK for their honeymoon, where she dragged him from one historical monument and castle to another.

A mother of three, her two little gentlemen in the making, a future lady (she hopes) keep her busy in the real world, but whenever she gets a moment's peace she loves to write romance novels in an array of genres, including regency, medieval and time travel.

Printed in Great Britain
by Amazon